AL...
HERE FOR YOU

'Truly gripping.'
Saffia Farr, Editor, JUNO Magazine

'A must-read of our times.'
WRD Magazine

'A heart-stopping portrayal. Essential reading for teens
and parents of teens – this book may well save lives.'
Angela Kiverstein

'A crucial read – current and compelling.'
Penny Joelson

'Poignant, powerful and educational.'
Emma Suffield,
SLA UK School Librarian of the Year 2018

'Impossible to put down.'
Lucas Maxwell, Portable Magic Dispenser

'A very important book.'
From Bee With Love

ALWAYS
HERE FOR YOU

MIRIAM HALAHMY

First published in the UK in 2020 by ZunTold
www.zuntold.com

Text copyright © Miriam Halahmy 2019
Cover design by Sophie Standing

A catalogue record for this book is available
from the British Library

ISBN 978-1-9162042-1-8
1 2 3 4 5 6 7 8 9 10

Printed and bound in the UK by
Short Run Press Limited
25 Bittern Road
Sowton Industrial Estate
EXETER
Devon
EX2 7LW

Chapter 1
Alone

Holly woke with a start. The doorbell was ringing and ringing; an impatient ding dong echoing through the house.

Mum'll answer, she told herself, her eyes heavy with sleep.

But there was no sound of Mum's heels tapping down the hallway to the front door, or Dad's cheery voice calling from the kitchen.

Two loud bangs, as if someone was slamming the door with the flat of their hand and more impatient ringing.

Holly rolled over, waiting for the person to give up and go away.

Silence strained up the stairs and around the bedroom door.

No-one's home, she thought. The house is empty. Again.

Between half open curtains Holly could see dense clouds spreading across a grey February sky. It was another gloomy Saturday morning and probably freezing cold on the beach. The waves would be pounding on the pebbles by now and crashing up against the girders of the pier. The red digits on her bedside clock winked 10:16... 10:17... 10:18... Her ears felt deadened with the silence.

I could lie here all day alone, Holly thought, with a shiver.

That made her throw back the covers, slip into pumps and a hoody and go downstairs.

Their house was the only detached one in a street of old houses looming up on either side. Tall dense trees framed the back garden, blocking light from the kitchen. There was only sun at the front of the house and only in the mornings. Holly hadn't really noticed in the past how dark their house was but now she was always peering into shadowy corners.

At the bottom of the stairs, she padded to the front door and peered through the square glass panel. There was no-one outside so she opened the door. Propped up against the potted fern on the step was an Amazon parcel.

Just a delivery man, she told herself, flicking her hair back.

Holly picked up the parcel. It looked like Mum's book for her book group meeting this month.

Going back inside, she closed the front door and went down the hall to the kitchen. The big window was streaming with rain and she could hardly see the garden. It made her feel even more lonely.

If Amy was still in the house opposite she could run over in her shorts and hoody. Amy would still be in bed and she could climb in with her. They'd lie there giggling and listen to music, sharing Amy's earphones.

Amy's Mum would bring up tea and toast and they'd sit up in bed and straighten each other's hair, Holly's shoulder length and dark brown, Amy's blonde and longer.

Amy had asked for straighteners when they were twelve and taught Holly how to use them, her green eyes serious as she quoted their favourite YouTube stylist, eighteen-year-old Sandi.

"Sandi says you don't have to spend all day to look good," Amy would say. "Straighteners take no time. Sandi says hair's everything."

Holly had nodded and asked for straighteners for *her* twelfth birthday, two months later. Ever since she made sure her hair was always straight and gleaming.

Amy was a few centimetres taller than Holly and could run faster on her long thin legs but they both hated sports, especially swimming.

"Messes up your hair," said Amy.

Fortunately, their High School didn't offer swimming.

But they both loved collecting old stuff. Amy's speciality was china and Holly's was small pretty objects. Most of her collection was stored in a large shoe box. She had a load of different teaspoons – too many Amy said, rolling her eyes – bits of dolls' tea sets, especially a dinky teapot with a cracked spout; all sorts of rings and those little tin boxes which might have held sweeteners or maybe snuff – whatever that was.

"At least your stuff doesn't take up too much room," Amy would say, tossing back her hair so that it fell down her back.

"Not like all your jugs and teacups," Holly would say, her grey eyes crinkled in a grin.

Somehow, Amy always managed to look older than Holly, even when they both followed Sandi's advice together. Holly's cheeks were still chubby like in Primary School; she didn't have that clearly defined chin and profile like Amy.

It doesn't really matter, Holly told herself. We'll always be best friends.

But then, last December, Amy and her family had moved to Canada, leaving Holly all alone in school and in the past few weeks, since Gran's Crisis, more and more often alone in the house.

"Now you're fourteen, its OK, isn't it?" Mum had said, the first time Gran locked herself out of the house. It was a dark January evening, already gone six and Dad wouldn't be home for at least an hour. "Finish your essay and I'll be back before you know it."

Holly had nodded and shrugged as if she didn't care. That was what Mum expected. But the silence which folded around her worried her more than she wanted to admit.

Who's scared to be left alone for a couple of hours at fourteen? she asked herself.

Amy, came the answer. Only if Amy was here, it'd be OK.

But Amy was gone.

Now as Holly walked across the kitchen she saw the usual note propped up against the kettle.

Dad at the office. I'm taking Gran to do a big shop. Back this afternoon. Takeaway tonight. You choose xx Mum

Dad headed up a busy accountancy firm and was often tied up with clients late into the evening and sometimes on Saturdays. Mum worked part-time as a receptionist at a doctor's surgery but more and more often she was at Gran's house these days, coping with the latest crisis.

Or in this case, the weekly shopping, thought Holly.

She stared at the takeaway menus on the counter.

As if my whole Saturday is about food, she thought.

There was a loud creak behind her and she swivelled.

Someone's there, she thought, heart pumping away.

There was a second creak.

Is it Mum?

Feeling a bit wobbly, she crept out of the kitchen into the hall. A draught caught her bare legs and two loud creaks made her jump. Then she saw the living room door swing.

"It's nothing," she said aloud to herself.

The living room door creaked again. She looked around for something to wedge it and spotted the flat iron. Mum liked to collect old stuff, something she and Holly used to do together when Holly was little. The flat iron was heavy, one of those irons they used to heat on an open fire or later on a gas jet.

Holly remembered when they'd bought it years ago. She was eleven and no-one would have dreamt of leaving her alone in the house then.

She and Mum had been wandering down North Laines, a warren of narrow streets in Brighton famous for vintage and junk shops, cheaper than the more touristy Lanes nearer the beach. They lived in Clifton, a few minutes' bus ride from Brighton centre.

It was Mum who spotted the iron and called Holly over. "Look at that, I love it."

Holly had picked it up and nearly dropped it. "Wow! It's so heavy."

"Yes, solid iron, we'll have it."

They'd brought it home and left it on the hall table along with the clown made from Venetian glass and a silver hairbrush and mirror set Mum had inherited from her grandmother.

Now Holly pushed the annoying living room door flat against the wall and settled the iron against the wood.

Back in the kitchen the wall clock said 10:46.

Her phone was on the counter. She checked her messages. Nothing much except one from Amy sent yesterday Canadian time.

There was a snap of her friend in a closely fitted, designer snow suit and next to her was a tall blond boy wearing a dark red ski jacket. The boy had his arm around Amy's shoulders and they were both smiling, their teeth as dazzling as the sunlit snow all around them.

gabe says hi

He's gorgeous, thought Holly with a pang. She'd no idea what to send back. A selfie in my hoody? she wondered. In the end she snapped the kettle and messaged,

he looks nice any vintage shops in canada

Maybe remembering their shopping trips would remind Amy that once they were the very best of friends. Since nursery, thought Holly, as she stared out at the dripping garden.

I'm off to the shops, she decided with a jolt. Even in the rain it was better than hanging at home, jumping at every sound.

Twenty minutes later, showered, dressed and huddled into her old jacket she was standing at the bus stop.

Holly had lived in Brighton all her life and she and Amy loved it; the shops, the cafés, the students in term time swigging beer and running night clubs on the beach, the Mall at Churchill Square where they would hang on wet days, the pier full of kiosks and slot machines and the pebbly beaches where they sunbathed on hot days.

As she stepped off the bus the rain was even heavier and she felt water leak along the seam of her hood. Have to remind Mum I need a new jacket, she thought and set off at a rapid pace towards her favourite shops. Dodging into Harry's Emporium and dragging her hood down, she felt herself cheer up for the first time that morning. All around her were glass cases crammed with old china and medals, shelves bulging with tempting junk and racks of hangers full of vintage clothes.

No-one knows where I am or cares, she thought. She had her headphones in, music blasting out, when the bass suddenly reminded her how her heart had thumped when she heard the living room door creak.

Wasn't this the shop where she'd seen the torch alarm? She and Amy had dug it out of a crate of old musty stuff and passed it between them, giggling about setting it off in class. But then Amy had accidentally pressed the button and the most horrible, piercing sound filled their ears.

Grumpy Harry, the shop owner, with greasy hair and a shabby suit jacket that didn't match his trousers, had come over and grabbed it from them, barking out, "Go on, get out you kids, scaring off my customers!"

Now Holly thought, Maybe I should get an alarm like that, keep it by the front door just in case. That would scare anyone nasty off or alert the police.

For a minute she let her imagination run wild with pictures of police cars rushing to her rescue, sirens wailing. Then the song changed to a slow one and she came back down to earth.

You're crazy, Holly Bennett, she told herself. How would the police hear an alarm inside the house? You'd have to phone them first and they'd take ages to arrive.

She pulled up her hood, walked back outside and further down the street. She was looking for a tiny shop which opened up after Amy left. Maybe they have some new stuff, she thought, but then she noticed Noah Levy across the road and he was with gorgeous Rick Gold. Both boys were in her school.

Noah was a few centimetres shorter than Holly with skinny legs and a pale face. His hair stuck up on the top of his head. Back in Year 7 when they were only eleven, he often looked ready to burst into tears. Amy used to roll her eyes which made Holly grin back. She felt close to tears herself in those first weeks at High School.

She would never have coped without Amy. Her best friend always went first, leading the way in all their games and smoothing the path through Primary School right up to Year 9. All she'd ever needed was her one good friend. Then Amy told her about Canada. It was the worst moment of her life.

She shook herself and stared over at the boys. Noah's mum was in the same book group as Holly's mum and they lived a few streets away but Holly never hung out with Noah or anything.

She had a thing for Rick, however, which she hadn't even admitted to Amy. Rick was tall with broad shoulders and short fair hair. Noah barely came up to his shoulder. But Rick had never given Holly a second glance.

What if he notices me now, she thought. What should I say?

Oh, out shopping too? (How lame). Um – hey Rick, wassup? (Too gangsta).

Noah threw a look over his shoulder, his eyes wide as though he was scared or something.

Or he's about to cry, thought Holly. Now that is lame.

Then Rick put his hand on Noah's shoulder and the two of them stepped into a corner shop.

Rick Gold, thought Holly, with an inward sigh. He's easily as fit as Amy's skiboy, Gabe.

But why's he hanging with weepy Noah Levy?

Chapter 2
Madison and The Bezzies

It was still raining on Monday morning after a wet weekend stuck indoors with 'the olds' as Holly now called her parents. She'd heard Madison say it once and there was a satisfying frown from Mum when she threw it out at home.

The worst thing about Monday mornings was double PE. Holly hated changing in front of the other girls. One by one every single girl in her class seemed to have developed bodies with curves in all the right places.

Holly remained flat chested like in Primary School.

Now she tried to pull off her PE top and pull on her school shirt without anyone noticing.

"Still in a training bra, Holly," came Aisha's grating voice.

She was one of the Bezzies – Madison's best mates - which consisted of the prettiest and most popular girls in class.

"Holly's sooo young still," someone else said in a low voice and there was a general hum of agreement.

Holly went bright red as she fumbled with the buttons on her shirt. She swiftly pulled up her skirt, leaving the shirt hanging outside like the other girls and dropped her tie round her neck. Everyone kept their ties short, top shirt button undone, sleeves turned up twice to show off – in Madison's case – slender wrists. Holly's wrists were still chubby like her cheeks.

Madison threw her a kind smile. "Don't worry sweetie, you'll catch up one day."

Holly tried to smile back but her lips were dry and stuck together. She focused on slipping into her shoes.

Madison was the tallest girl in the class, with long fair hair, darkish threaded eyebrows, lips which pouted perfectly for a selfie and an underwired bra.

Holly had picked one of those up in the shops a week ago but Mum had taken it out of her hand, saying, 'You're not ready for that yet, darling.'

Madison was standing now in front of the mirror in her underwear, brushing her hair, turning her head from side and side – to make sure everyone's watching, Holly thought. She had that sort of fair skin which tanned an even gold in the summer.

Mum's skin tanned like that in the sun but Holly's pale skin, like Dad's, simply went red and she blushed scarlet at the tiniest thing. Mum was taller than Holly and almost four centimetres taller than Dad, 'with a great figure', Dad was always saying with his comfortable grin.

Holly took after Dad's side of the family and despaired of ever looking remotely attractive.

She'd known Madison since nursery, like Amy, but she'd

never been one of her crowd. If she saw Madison or any of the Bezzies in the Mall they'd blow kisses but they'd never invite her to hang with them. Madison wasn't mean or anything but she and Amy didn't have much to do with her.

Only these days, since Amy had gone, the exclusion zone made Holly feel even more lonely.

Madison's phone pinged. Everyone looked round in case the teacher heard but she was out of the room.

Madison grabbed the phone, checked it and called out, "It's Harry!"

"What's he say? Show me, show me," called out Aisha, running over.

The Bezzies all gathered round and Holly craned her neck but couldn't see the screen.

"He's so fit," said someone. "How did you meet?"

Holly knew Madison would love repeating the story.

"So," Madison said, as everyone gazed at her, "my cousin did a Shoutout and 'cos it's my cousin, I added him and you know how it is, we started messaging and sending snaps and he's so cute." She gave a deep sigh.

"Mmm, definitely cute," said someone.

Holly craned again and managed to see the top half of the screen. A boy with a long face and high cheekbones, older than her year group, longish light brown hair and wearing a green and gold rugby shirt, was standing on Brighton pier, grinning.

He looks nice, she thought with another inward sigh.

"So we said we'd meet up in the Mall on Saturday," went on Madison.

"Yeah and I had your back," said Aisha, flicking her long dark hair over her shoulders.

Aisha had smooth brown skin, dark hair which was thicker than Madison's and fell around her shoulders, and really long legs. She was a striker in the girls' football team and could push over most of the boys in their year.

Except perhaps Rick Gold, Holly couldn't help thinking.

Madison gave a giggle. "Course you did, babes. I mean, I'm not stupid."

General hum of agreement round the room.

We've had all the talks, thought Holly. About keeping safe online. Not that I'm going to meet anyone, online or offline, unless I go to Canada and hang with Amy. She's only been gone two months and she's already got a boyfriend.

A pang of jealousy went through her.

"His name's Harry, as you know," Madison was saying.

They all nodded and grinned.

"He's sixteen." She paused for effect.

Everyone looked very impressed.

"In Sixth Form College doing A levels and he wants to be a lawyer."

"Smart," muttered someone.

"Super smart," said Madison and she was flicking through her phone to show more photos when the door opened.

Miss Holland, the PE teacher, flew into the room, crying out, "Come on you lot, get a move on, it's lunchtime."

The Bezzies closed around Madison, giving her time to put her phone on silent and stuff it in her bag. Any phones found in class time were confiscated, sometimes until the end of term. 'A fate worse than death,' as Madison told everyone.

They finished dressing and poured out of the changing room talking non-stop about boys and sleepovers which Holly never seemed to be invited to.

Holly was the last one to arrive at the dining room, school bag hanging over her left arm. Part of her wished she still had a rucksack she could sling on her shoulder like last year.

But Madison had pronounced that, 'So Y7'.

No girl in Y9 would be seen dead with a rucksack now.

The dining room was heaving. Usually Holly managed to squeeze on the end of Madison's table with The Bezzies. But today the table was full and as she balanced her tray and her school bag she stared around the room, making small moves forward so she didn't look like she had no-one to sit with. More and more often now she found herself alone at lunchtime.

Then she spotted a chair on a table by the wall and walking over – not too fast, so she didn't look desperate – she was about to dump her tray when she saw Ellen on the other side.

Ellen rarely spoke, in class or out, but when she did it was usually something mean and mostly in a growly voice. Holly and Amy avoided her and wouldn't dream of sitting with her at lunch.

Ellen had red tangled hair which fell around her shoulders and looked as if it had never been brushed. Her uniform seemed too tight for her and her blazer was covered in some sort of animal hair.

Maybe she has pets, Holly thought now, with a

sinking feeling.

But there was nowhere else to sit.

"Anyone here?" she said, in a bright voice.

Ellen didn't answer or even look up. Her eyes were fixed on a plate of chips she was ploughing through.

Holly dumped her tray, pulled out a chair and sat down, her school bag sliding off her arm and landing upside down on the floor.

Ellen tutted without looking up and stuffed two fat chips in her mouth.

The room buzzed with chatter and as Holly picked up her cheese and cucumber sandwich, she could hear Madison's high-pitched giggle and Aisha's deeper laugh floating towards her. She tried to catch Madison's eye but failed.

Turning back, she watched Ellen scoop up more chips.

"Nice," she muttered, without catching Ellen's eye.

"You what?"

"Chips, I...er ... like chips, you know, with egg or sausage..."

"...what's it to you what I eat!" cut in Ellen.

"No, I didn't mean... it's just my Mum's always going on about healthy eating and stuff and..."

Holly stopped as Ellen narrowed her eyes, lowered her head – like a charging bull, thought Holly – and growled, "My mum's dead. Now will you shut up."

Holly felt herself go scarlet all the way down to her waist. You're such a loser Holly Bennett. You can't even sit at a table and chat to another girl without making a total mess of it. Who'd want to be friends with you?

She picked up her sandwich to take another bite when

she saw Tim Baker hovering, removing his earphones as he shifted from one foot to the other.

Tim was tall and very thin. His blazer didn't seem to fit either, Holly couldn't help noticing. The sleeves finished a few centimetres below the elbows. Tim's face was more freckles than red and it looked 'weathered' as Gran would say, like Grandad's face when he worked in the garden all summer. Tim wore a black beanie pulled low on his forehead and his longish hair curled out under it in all directions.

Holly stared up at him.

Ellen went on eating chips.

Tim fiddled with the wire hanging from his hand and coughed. "Er, that was good, um… what you said in English last Friday… about wanting to be a vet's nurse."

Ellen raised her head and her eyes lightened a bit. Holly could see they were a really clear blue. And she has proper cheekbones, just like Sandi, she thought, with a pang of envy. Makes her look so much older than me.

"Oh yes?" said Ellen.

Tim nodded. "I like animals."

"Uh huh."

"Yeah, you know, we keep chickens and goats and we've got dogs…"

"…how many?"

Tim coughed again. "Um, eight right now. One of them had a litter of six. They're cute." Tim's voice faded away.

There was a silence as Holly sucked on her juice.

Then Tim gave his little cough and said, "Better go."

As he sloped away, Ellen called out, "Laters."

Tim's shoulders straightened a tiny bit and then he plugged in his earphones before disappearing out of the room.

Lunch ended and lessons started again. Holly was left without a partner in Science and had to team up with two boys who talked about a computer game all the time. She did all the work but she didn't mind. At least in lessons there was structure and purpose. It was in the corridors and at lunchtime she didn't know how to be any more.

How do you get a new crowd? she puzzled to herself over and over, staring into the blue flame of the Bunsen burner. Amy and me were fine; we didn't need a crowd. But Amy's gone and now she's got a boyfriend.

It was sort of OK sitting with Ellen at lunch, she thought, with an inward sigh. Well it could be worse. And Tim Baker's nice. At least he's not noisy or dumb like most of the other boys. But is that making new friends? How do you know?

She suddenly felt so weary and adjusted the goggles on her nose. The boys giggled to each other, ignoring Holly, making her feel even more left out.

After school as she walked towards the street, she saw Tim pushing a mountain bike, his schoolbag strapped on the back. How far out of town does he live? she thought. He said his family kept all those animals. Do they have a farm?

Tim didn't notice her or if he did, he didn't nod or anything and Holly walked out of the school gate, alone as usual.

It was beginning to drizzle but she decided to avoid

the bus and walk the twenty-five minutes back to Clifton. Mum will be home, she told herself and dinner will be in the oven.

Chicken casserole on Monday nights. She couldn't wait, she was starving.

Chapter 3
zebrachats

It was after four when Holly arrived damp and chill at her front door. There was no sign of Mum's car.

Doesn't mean she's not home, she told herself, as she put her key in the lock and turned it. Maybe her car's in the garage, or Dad had to borrow it because he's got a flat tyre or...

But she knew the instant she stepped in the hallway. The house was cold and silent. The heating didn't come on until five. Even more telling, there were no cooking smells.

Holly dumped her schoolbag and coat and walked down to the kitchen. The door was wide open but the room was almost dark. The trees in the back garden were bending towards the kitchen window. Black clouds filled the sky. A storm was brewing out at sea and even up here in Clifton there'd be a rattling of windows and doors half the night. Foghorns were blasting away offshore, their mournful sound carried across town on the fierce wind.

Holly shivered and opened the oven door. She knew it was empty. The oven was cold; it hadn't been on today at all. Looking over to the kettle, she saw the note.

Gran's had a fall. Gone to the hospital xx Mum

Oh no! thought Holly, hands shaking as she pulled her phone out of her school bag. Poor Gran. But another thought came to her almost immediately. Does that mean Mum will be out even more?

That's a bit selfish, she told herself as Mum answered.

"Gran tripped over in the street," came her mother's voice through the speaker and she sounded tired. "Someone called an ambulance but it's not too bad. We're home now and she's resting up. She fell on her bad knee, it's quite bruised and even more swollen."

"Bring her over to stay with us," said Holly.

Mum gave a short laugh. "You know Gran, all independent. She won't do that!"

Holly felt her heart sink a bit. Then she had another thought. "Shall I find the emergency money and come over in a taxi? Help you out."

"No, darling. No need. We'll be all right but I'll stay over. Dad should be home soon. You'll be OK, won't you?" Mum's voice sounded concerned.

But not that much, Holly thought.

What could she say?

"Yep. Course. Give Gran my love."

Their phones disconnected and Holly was left alone in the silent kitchen, telling herself again that she was really quite selfish.

I just want everyone home with me. It's poor Gran who's hurt.

* * *

At 73 Gran had been struggling with a bad knee for a couple of years, not helped by the fact she'd never learned to drive.

"Never needed to, Holly, darling," she used to say.

Grandad had driven them everywhere. They lived about 45 minutes from Brighton; there was a shop and a Post Office in the village and a good bus service into town.

"That's all we need," Gran used to say in her cheerful voice.

Holly knew Gran couldn't cope with long walks anymore. They had a dog, Lucy, a golden Labrador and before the bad knee, they used to walk her miles across the Downs every day.

"Your Grandad has to drive me to the top now to see the views," Gran would say with a grin.

Lucy was the only animal Holly had ever liked. Dad didn't like any animals because he was allergic and Holly was scared of sharp teeth and claws which most of them had.

Grandad never said much, just nodded and smiled in agreement when Gran said anything. But Grandad had died last November and poor dear Lucy had died a week later.

"She was broken-hearted, like me," Gran had said, her eyes dark with tears and sorrow.

As Holly listened to her grandmother, wiping her own tears away, she had felt as though their lives were entering some strange new territory.

How do you suddenly start living your life all alone? she'd wondered as she stared into Gran's sad eyes.

"Forty-six years we were married," Gran kept saying.

"Nothing's the same now. Even the air smells different without your Grandad."

Mum's parents were the only grandparents Holly had ever known. Her other set of grandparents had died when she was a baby. She loved being with Gran and Grandad, often staying in the holidays with them when Mum was working. Sometimes Amy came too and they were allowed to make camps in the wood at the end of the garden. The best thing was when Grandad made a camp fire and they roasted potatoes and marshmallows and were allowed to stay up really late. The sky would go black above them and they could see the stars. Holly was never afraid in the dark then because everyone was with her. Wood smoke became one of Holly's favourite smells, along with the scent of Amy's facial peach scrub.

"Sandi says soap is a nightmare on the skin," Amy told her. "Never ever use soap on your face."

After Grandad's funeral, which was so horrible Holly thought she could never be as sad again, Gran seemed to go to pieces. She sat in the living room crying and crying and Mum and Dad decided she couldn't stay at home alone. So Dad drove her all the way to Aberdeen to stay with Uncle Henry, Mum's big brother, and Aunty Mo and Holly's older cousins. Gran settled down and seemed much more cheerful. She stayed until New Year – six weeks ago.

Then she got 'a bee in her bonnet' as Mum kept saying through gritted teeth.

"I decided to come back home and go it alone," Gran said to Holly over Sunday lunch after Dad brought her back.

Gran was quite a tall person although Mum was taller. Her hair had been the same colour as Mum's but now was mostly white. She had the same dark eyebrows and brown eyes and like Mum her skin tanned really well.

But going it alone had meant crisis after crisis. Gran lost her keys and had forgotten to leave a spare set with the neighbours; her credit card was swallowed by a cash machine and she was too scared to go in and tell the bank; she had a fall at home and bruised her ribs – not serious, but she refused to let Mum bring carers in to help her.

Hardly a day had gone by in the past few weeks without something going wrong, usually in the evening when either Mum or Dad already had something important on and that meant one parent dashing off to rescue Gran and the other out until late.

"You're fourteen, old enough to be left alone in the house for a bit, aren't you darling?" Mum kept saying.

"Course she is, stop fussing," Dad would say, his eyes crinkling up in one of his comfortable grins.

When Dad grinned Holly usually felt grown up and sensible.

But being left alone in the house seemed to bother her more and more.

If only Gran's Crisis was over and we could get back to normal, she told herself every day.

Now as wind lashed rain against the darkening window and the house creaked and cracked around her, Holly wished again that she'd bought a torch alarm, like the one she'd seen last year in the junk shop.

If I just had it to hand, she thought, I'd feel a bit braver.

It was nearly five, she had no idea when Dad would be home and she was starving. She tuned the radio to her favourite station and rummaging in the freezer, pulled out an individual pizza and a bag of oven chips. There was a tub of Belgian chocolate ice cream which Mum had been saving for a special occasion.

She hesitated for a moment and then with a shrug. she thought, Who cares? Anyway, there's no-one here to stop me.

Switching the oven on, she put in a large portion of chips and the pizza.

The heating had come on and as the house began to warm up and the smell of cooking leaked out of the oven, Holly raced upstairs, checked no-one was lurking in the bedrooms and changed into a long-sleeved T and leggings. Leaving her feet bare she went back down, grabbed her school bag, put on all the lights in the living room and the hall and went back to the kitchen.

Homework, she told herself with satisfaction, spreading her books out across the counter.

Holly didn't have a favourite subject at school and neither had Amy. They both liked lessons and always got good grades. They often did homework together – "but not copying," Amy said, Holly nodding in her serious way.

"It doesn't matter if we don't know what we want to do now," Amy was always saying.

"Course not," Holly had agreed.

"Once we get to Sixth Form, we can make a choice and then we can go to uni together and share a flat. We can bring all the things we bought in the junk shops."

But now Amy had a boyfriend and, if she was honest, it felt as though all the girls at school were growing away from her and going out with boys. How am I supposed to keep up? Holly asked herself.

With a sigh she turned back to Science homework.

She watched a YouTube video as she ate the chips and pizza. Sandi was giving tips on eye make-up. Holly thought it looked complicated.

She didn't bother with a plate or cutlery just picked everything up in her fingers.

If Amy were here we'd have such a laugh without the olds around. But there's no-one here and maybe there won't be for ages until Gran feels better.

The thought made her sad and she went and pulled the ice cream out of the freezer. It was full.

Do I dare eat it straight from the tub? she wondered.

Yes I do! she told herself and dumped it onto the counter to soften while she finished the chips.

By eight Holly had eaten half the ice cream and was feeling a bit sick. She'd also finished all her homework but still no sign of Dad. The storm was raging round the house now and every sound made her jump.

Her phone pinged. It was from Amy. There was a new snap of herself with three girls lying in a heap on a crumpled bed, all dressed in shorts and strappy tops.

Sleepover, thought Holly, with a deep pang of envy.

Then a second snap appeared. It was Amy and Gabe sharing a chocolate milkshake in a café, grinning at each other as they sucked on straws.

There was a short message:-

i luv canada

Not surprising, thought Holly with a hollow feeling inside her. Amy's messages made her feel even more out of things.

Everyone has a boyfriend except me, Holly thought. If I had a boyfriend I wouldn't feel so lonely when I'm home all alone. We could message each other and stuff. Hang out, like the other girls do. They were always going on about how they'd stayed up half the night messaging each other.

Sort of like a sleepover, Holly decided. Wish I had someone like that.

She stared at the remains of her dinner lying over the counter; the spoon stuck up in the melting ice cream.

"Don't see why I can't have a boyfriend too," she said out loud.

Her laptop was open on the counter. She grabbed the mouse and moved the pointer to the search engine.

Madison and Aisha were talking about chatrooms in school that afternoon. They were always meeting boys and chatting to them. You had to be careful of course, they all knew that.

"But they can't jump out the screen at you," Aisha had said. "If we see something we don't like we just say, Bye and unhook, right?"

zebrachats – that was the name of the chatroom they used.

Holly typed *zebrachats* into the search engine and it came up straight away.

Cool, she thought and typed in her username, *stardust16*, the age she wanted to be.

stardust16 has joined the chat room appeared on the screen and chats started to stream.

Holly scrolled through and then someone messaged her:-

george10: hi stardust16
stardust16: hi george
george10: RU doing reading or maths homework

Holly stared at the screen, puzzled. What does he mean?

stardust16: science
        : U in y9?
george10: y6 im 10 how old RU?

Holly felt herself go red. She was talking to a little kid. How sad is that? How did he even get into the chat room at his age? She remembered Aisha's tip.

stardust16: 16 sweetie bye now

It actually felt good calling a little kid sweetie.

Holly carried on reading messages down the screen and then someone else buzzed her:-

jimmycoolguy: wassup star

That's more like it, thought Holly.

stardust16: not much U?

jimmycoolguy: Y11 so much pressure

stardust16: yep me 2

jimmycoolguy: good 2 chat an take a break

stardust16: great

This is really good, thought Holly. As they chatted on and on, he kept telling her how much he liked her and how much he'd like to hook up. He lived in London. She didn't say she was in Brighton – Aisha's warning voice was in her ear – they can't jump out of the screen but you have to be careful. An hour sped by before she knew it and she hadn't thought once about being home alone.

jimmycoolguy: trying to imagine what u look like
                 babes
              : grey eyes just guessing u know

stardust16: cool yep thats me

jimmycoolguy: wow brainbox aint i? blonde frizzy hair?

stardust16: haha no straight light brown

jimmycoolguy: send me a pic huh

Holly hesitated. What would Aisha do?

jimmycoolguy: still there?

stardust16: yep

There was the ping of a snap coming on the screen. Holly stared at it for a second, not really understanding. She could see the bare torso of a teenage boy from the neck down and the waistband of his jeans pulled low.

Holly wasn't sure why she felt shocked. After all she saw boys without their tops at the swimming pool. But somehow this was different – creepy.

Her hand hovered over the mouse as another message appeared.

jimmycoolguy: nice huh?? now U

              : keep UR bra on this time if U want babes

This time? Is he mad? Shaking with fear as if the boy was going to come through the front door, she logged off and pushed the laptop across the counter.

No wonder Aisha and Madison only went on chatrooms together.

The rain slammed against the window. The clock showed 21:14. No sign of Dad and no-one to laugh and gossip with about horrid Jimmy.

You'd never guess what just happened.

No way.

Way.

Loneliness settled like a cold stone in the pit of her stomach.

Chapter 4
Shoutout

Wednesday lunchtime Holly walked over to Ellen's table as she'd done all week. Madison seemed to have swelled the Bezzies to fill an entire table now and there was no room for hangers on.

Ellen had a double portion of chips in front of her. She didn't look up as Holly slid into the seat opposite with a bright smile, trying to look as if she always sat there.

Holly was tired; her eyes drooped as she unwrapped her egg sandwich. Dad had gone away on business and Mum had messaged to say she might be late home again. Holly didn't like to go to bed until Mum was home.

As she reached for her juice carton, Tim Baker arrived and sat down next to Ellen. To Holly's amazement Ellen offered Tim a chip.

"Thanks," he said, scooping up a couple. He took out his phone and swiped. "This is Mabel," he said, showing Ellen the screen.

"Ahhh," mumbled Ellen, her mouth full.

Tim shot her a grin and said, "She's nearly six. I think

she wants to be a dog, you know."

"Follows you around?" said Ellen.

"Everywhere I go," said Tim. "Plus she loves the pups." He swiped again.

"Oh that's so sweet," said Ellen, with a little laugh.

"Wanna see?" Tim turned the phone to Holly.

A wave of gratitude washed through her. When was the last time someone had included her in anything?

The snap showed a goat licking a furry mound of golden Labrador puppies.

Sick, she thought, but she forced a smile. "Nice."

"You got any pets?" Tim asked Holly.

"No, my Dad's allergic. But they look, um, sweet."

These two were seriously crazy about animals so she had to make an effort. There was nowhere else to sit at lunch.

Tim gave a sympathetic smile.

Then Holly's phone pinged. It was a message from Mum.

Still at Gran's. Water dripping through kitchen ceiling. Worried you haven't had proper dinner all week so asked Linda Levy if you could go there. Walk home with Noah. Sorry darling. Make it up to you at the weekend. Get that new jacket. xxxxxxxxxxxxx Mum

Holly stared at the screen in complete horror. How much worse could her life get? She wasn't really sure if Tim and Ellen were actually her friends now – they'd only sat together for lunch twice – and now she had to go home with Noah.

"Bad news?" asked Tim in his kind voice.

Holly looked up. Ellen was giving her a hard stare.

Holly shrugged and said, "Nah, just the olds."

Tim rolled his eyes and stood up to leave, reaching for the earphone wire.

"Laters," he said.

"Laters," said Ellen, with her tiny smile.

Holly watched him slope off, woolly hat pulled low on his forehead.

It looked like Tim was joining them at lunch but that was only because of Ellen.

Who cares? she told herself but inside she felt like the last chip on the plate, abandoned, too greasy to be desired.

The rest of lunchbreak Holly sat in the library. Then it was double maths and as she came out of class at the end the day, Noah entered the corridor.

Their eyes met and Holly looked away but Noah came over and said in a quiet voice, "See you on the corner."

She gave a brief nod and he disappeared into the crowd.

At least he didn't expect them to walk out of the school gates together in full view of the entire school.

It took Holly about ten minutes to retrieve homework from her locker and walk off to the end of the road. Noah was waiting under a tree.

"Walk or bus?" said Noah.

"Walk." If they caught the bus there were bound to be other kids from school they knew.

As they set off, Noah pulled up the hood of his jacket and shoved his hands in his pockets. His legs were so thin his grey school trousers flapped about in the wind.

They walked all the way to Clifton and past the end of Holly's street in silence.

Holly couldn't help wondering if maybe something good could come out of this. Noah hung with Rick, didn't he?

Just as they reached Noah's street, she said in a casual voice, "Didn't know you went round with Rick Gold."

Noah stopped in his tracks so suddenly Holly nearly tripped over him.

"Watch it!" she cried out.

"I don't," said Noah, his eyes scanning her face.

"Don't what?"

"Go round with him." He was glancing over his shoulder as if they were being followed.

"I saw you," said Holly. "You went into a shop with Rick."

"No, look, you got it all wrong," blustered Noah.

Holly frowned and shook her head. "I don't get it. I saw you."

Noah pulled a bit of paper towel out of his pocket and blew his nose. His cheeks had gone red but the rest of his face was very pale.

He's not going to cry, is he? thought Holly.

"Don't say anything at home," said Noah, pushing the paper towel into his pocket. "My parents, they wouldn't understand and the twins – they're just dumb. Promise me, please Holly."

Noah sounded so frightened Holly couldn't help feeling sorry for him.

"OK."

A look of relief crossed Noah's face. "Thanks," he said in a small voice.

"S'alright," said Holly.

She followed Noah up the street and hovered on the doorstep as he turned the key in the lock.

"I'm home," he called out, as they stepped into a square light hall.

There was a smell of baking and Holly felt wrapped up in warmth. They must have had the heating on all day, she thought.

"Hello love. Holly with you?" came the voice of a woman from the back of the house.

"Yes." Noah turned to Holly and said, "Hang your coat up here and dump your bag."

He looked up as two older boys came clattering downstairs.

"Hey bruv, nice chick. I'm Adam," the tallest of the two said, a sly grin on his face. "This is Sam."

Both boys were at least fifteen with brown curly hair, darker than Noah's. Adam was taller and chunkier than Sam.

"Holly, meet the twins," said Noah, in a grudging voice.

"So how long you two been an item?" asked Adam.

"Yeah, yeah," Sam said as Holly frowned.

She started to say, "You have to be jo…" when she caught sight of Noah's face, even more miserable than when he pleaded with her in the street about Rick.

She stopped herself just in time.

Noah's mum, Linda, appeared in the hallway with a teacloth over her shoulder. "Right, everyone," she called out in a welcoming voice. "Sit down, dinner's ready. We eat early in this house, Holly, hope that's OK. Boys can't wait, you know?" She gave Holly a wink and Holly grinned back.

Linda was taller than the twins, with short wavy hair and they all had the same olive skin. She kept up a steady banter over home-made lasagne and salad, with crusty garlic bread. It was the best meal Holly had eaten all week.

"How's your gran doing?" Linda asked, as she flicked her teacloth at Adam who was trying to swipe Noah's garlic bread.

"Her knee's quite bad and Mum's worried about her all the time. Well, we all are," said Holly, blushing. Then she said in a bright voice, "This lasagne's delicious."

Linda gave her a warm smile and then the phone rang in the kitchen. She pushed her chair back and went off to answer it.

Noah shot her his nervous look as if scared at being left alone with the twins.

"You two going out tonight?" said Adam, with a snort.

"Yeah, yeah," said Sam, his lip curled up in a mocking grin.

"Just ignore them," muttered Noah.

Linda came back and the conversation turned to Cousin Ben's barmitzvah the Saturday after next.

"Noah's got to make a speech," said Adam and he and Sam exchanged grins.

"That's enough," said Linda with a frown. "Ever been to a barmitzvah, Holly?"

"No. It's for boys, isn't it?" said Holly, struggling to remember something from school. "When they're thirteen, or is it fourteen?"

"Thirteen and the girls do a batmitzvah. Equality and all that, you know."

Sam and Adam exchanged gagging sounds and

Linda said with a sigh, "It's so nice having another girl in the house." She rolled her eyes at Holly. "I'm always outnumbered."

Holly threw her a sympathetic smile. "So what do you do at a barmitzvah?"

"Read in Hebrew in front of the congregation, you're supposed to sing actually," said Linda. "They have to study hard for it."

"You should've heard Noah last year. His voice kept squeaking," said Sam through a mouthful of lasagne.

Both twins dissolved in mocking laughter and Linda looked from one to the other, shaking her head.

Why doesn't she tell them off? thought Holly.

Noah's ears had gone very red and he looked like he wanted to bury his head in his plate.

Adam play-punched Sam on the arm who choked and then spat out a mouthful of mush onto the tablecloth.

"Pack it in you two!" said Linda, but Adam banged Sam on the back so hard the table shook.

Linda turned back to Holly and said, "Once they've done their barmitzvah then they become an adult in the eyes of Jewish law."

"Only Noah missed that bit out. Eh bruv?" put in Adam.

Sam let out a mean snort.

Noah looked close to tears and Linda gave an exasperated sigh.

So this is life in a big family, thought Holly. At least when I'm alone there's no-one to tease me.

The twins went back to eating and Linda said to Holly in a bright voice, "It's quite an honour for Noah to be asked to make a speech, isn't it darling?"

Noah didn't look up and Linda went off to get dessert.

Adam waited until she was gone and then he said, "So how old are you, Holl, babes?"

"What?" said Holly, starting to go red again.

"She's in my year you muppets," said Noah.

The twins both snorted at exactly the same time and then bumped fists.

Holly went an even deeper shade of red and Noah seemed helpless next to them.

"I was just thinking," Adam went on, as the twins stared Holly down, "You know those eleven-year-old kids who get put up years at school because they're child geniuses?" His voice was even more mocking than before.

Holly wanted to reach across and slap his face hard.

"We thought maybe you're one of them."

"You think I'm eleven!" Holly snapped and now her eyes pricked with tears.

Will no-one ever see me as growing up? she thought.

She was saved by the front door slamming and the appearance in the doorway of an older boy – eighteen? Holly thought – wearing a blue shirt and jeans. He had broad shoulders, short hair and pale skin like Noah. The boy took in the room at a glance and then narrowed his eyes at the twins.

They didn't even smirk back, Holly noted.

"Hey, Gideon," called out Noah in a relieved voice and he and Gideon bumped fists.

"All right?" said Gideon, nodding to Holly.

"This is Noah's girl…" started Adam

"… shut it twinbo," snapped Gideon and Adam coloured a deep red.

Yesss!! thought Holly.

Linda brought in a plate for Gideon and she also seemed relieved he'd arrived. Noah even spoke up about his speech which he was clearly dreading. Gideon gave him an encouraging smile.

The twins said very little and excused themselves early.

Holly had a second helping of apple pie and ice cream and listened to Gideon and Linda chat about their day while Noah nodded at everything his older brother said.

This is more like it, she thought.

Then Linda said, "Noah, take Holly upstairs and listen to your music if you like."

No way! thought Holly and a look of horror washed across Noah's face too.

"Oh no, sorry, thank you Mrs Levy," she said, pushing her chair back. "I have to go home and… um… find a book I need for my homework."

"Oh, that's a shame," said Linda, although it was clear to Holly that no-one else was bothered.

There was a bit of a discussion but Holly was insistent and in the end Gideon drove her back. It was past eight and dark outside.

"Want me to come in?" he said. "Check all's good in the house."

She could tell by his tone he was only being polite. "No, I'm fine. Thanks for the lift. Bye."

She heard the car drive away as she went up to the front door, opened it and stepped inside. No-one was home and the house seemed even darker than usual.

Holly changed out of her uniform, checking every room,

including the under-stairs cupboard. She rattled the locks on the patio doors and the front door twice each.

Then she laid out her homework on the kitchen counter and stared at her laptop.

The clock read 8:33.

Her phone pinged. It was a snap from Amy in the middle of a group of boys and girls standing knee deep in snow.

Amy's Canadian crowd, Holly thought, a sour taste in her mouth.

She didn't message back.

Twenty minutes later her phone pinged again. It was a Shoutout from Becca Wilson, one of the girls at school.

becca: hey everyone meet Jay nice funny guy

Holly checked Jay's profile. A couple of the girls at school had added Jay and his avatar was nice. He was already friends with Amy. So he must be OK, she told herself.

She thought back to the chatroom and the horrid snap *jimmycoolguy* had sent. A shudder went through her. Avatars were so much better, more private. Holly had spent ages creating her avatar.

Jay's had a cute grin on his.

Why not? she thought and added him.

A minute later her phone pinged. It was Jay.

jay : hey holly wanna hang

Chapter 5
Jay

holly: hey jay
jay: like UR avatar pretty hair
holly: thanks
jay : what U doing
holly: nothing home alone bored
jay: yeah me 2 mum out as usual
holly: and UR dad
jay: disappeared years ago
holly: oh sorry
jay: *smily emoji * its ok im used 2 it
holly: hang on
jay: what??
holly: thought i heard something back in a sec

Holly poked her head into the hallway, holding her breath, listening. Was that someone outside the front door?

"Mum," she called out in a small voice.

The living room door creaked quietly. It was almost ten. Why was no-one home?

She looked back at her phone, face up on the counter. Messages streamed down the screen. Walking over she grabbed it.

Jay was messaging how worried he was. That's cute, she thought.

jay: are U there?? be careful holly dont take any risks
holly: im here door creaking!! so hate being home alone
jay: me 2 totally hate it
holly: no way
jay: way

Holly laughed aloud and she felt her body relax as she sat back down at the kitchen table with her phone.

jay: sometimes i imagine im spiderman hanging from the ceiling keeping watch
holly: if UR spiderman what am i
jay: really really nice girl
holly: *shy embarrassed emoji*
jay: so glad i met U
holly: me too
    : U friends with amy?
jay: yeah friend of URS?
holly: best friend but gone 2 canada
jay: oh sorry miss her??
holly: yep
jay: me 2 my best friend gone
holly: oh
jay: yeah missing him
holly: horrible isn't it?
jay: yeah

: his name was mike
holly: did he move away

There was quite a long pause and Holly wondered if she'd said the wrong thing. But what could be bad about asking that. Then her screen lit up.

jay is typing...

jay: mike died

Holly let out a gasp and stared at the screen in horror. Dead! OMG. What if Amy was dead? The thought made her shiver. At least Amy's safe even if she's thousands of miles away in Canada, she told herself.

jay   : U still there??
holly: yep
       : sorry
       : dont know what 2 say
Jay: sorry holly
     : stupid stupid me
     : must have been a shock
holly: bigger shock 2 U
jay: UR so sweet

There was another pause. Holly stared at the screen trying to imagine how it would feel to go to Amy's funeral. Her mind was wandering over the music they might play when Jay started typing again.

jay: mike was killed in a car accident

      : really bad

      : everyone crying at the funeral

      : so bad

holly: *sad emoji* dont no how UR coping

jay: nearly a year ago getting better

      : when did amy leave??

holly: just after new year

      : six weeks tomorrow

jay: but she can message U

holly: amy hardly ever messages she sends pics of her
         boyfriend

jay: oh god

holly: yep makes me feel kinda left out

jay: course!! not very kind of her

holly: shes good friend

jay: course yeah course she is

holly: on my own a lot at school dont think she gets it

jay: should understand if shes good mate

holly: no one 2 hang with now

jay: yep know how it feels

      : all alone now

holly: like me

jay: yep

Mum appeared at the kitchen door. "Oh here you are! I've been calling out. Didn't you hear me?"

Holly looked up and for a moment couldn't focus.

Mum stared back at her, face puzzled, handbag tucked under her arm. She was wearing a loose long-sleeved top which was creased and there were tired lines under her eyes.

Holly shook her head to clear it and forced a grin

on her face. She didn't want to tell Mum who she was talking to. Not yet, she told herself.

"Just chatting," she said, swinging her phone in her hand. "How's Gran?"

Holly listened as Mum chattered on about Gran's problems and how worried she was but for once Holly found herself tuning out. All she really wanted to do was escape to her room and go on chatting to Jay. She hadn't felt so excited about anything for weeks.

Mum boiled the kettle while she talked and made them both tea.

Holly muttered her thanks, eyes glued to the screen.

jay: whens UR birthday
holly: jan 26
jay: no way im jan 25

Holly hesitated. Should she tell him old she really was, or lie like when she was stardust16? She decided to take the risk and a thrill went through her. When was the last time she felt so fizzy and fired up?

holly: im 14
jay: wow me 2!! fave colour?
holly: blue
jay: snap!! pets?
holly: hate animals all my family same
jay: OMG us 2!! never had pets *tongue out emoji*
holly: *scream emoji*
    : luv emojis
jay : *cartoon sticker: boy shouting YES!*

Holly laughed out loud.

"What is it, darling?" Mum called out from the other side of the table.

Holly looked up as if emerging from a dream. Mum was grinning at her, buttering toast and laying it out on plates for both of them. Her phone was on the table next to her and before Holly could say anything it pinged.

Mum stared at the screen. "It's Dad. Oh rats! He won't be home tonight after all. He's too tired to drive so he's stopped over in a hotel."

"Uh huh," murmured Holly. She was scrolling through the cartoon stickers looking for a good one to send back to Jay.

"Found it!" she said out loud.

holly: *sticker, grinning girl saying Giggle*
jay: U rock

"Earth to Holly!" It was Mum. "Focus please. How was dinner at the Levys?"

"OK." Holly didn't look up from the screen. Messages from Jay poured in and she could hardly keep up. If only Mum would go to bed or something.

"Did they talk about the barmitzvah? Linda told me all about it. Her sister's youngest, Ben. Linda had to get all the boys new suits. Of course, she's been through it four times already." Mum finished with a laugh.

Holly nodded, shoulders hunched, eyes down, tapping her screen.

"What did she make for dinner?" Mum went on, as she poured tea. "She's such a good cook, always bakes a cake for book group."

"Lasagne," muttered Holly, without looking up.

"They don't keep kosher or anything, Linda says they're modern Jewish," said Mum. "Holly? Are you listening?"

"Mmm," said Holly.

"But they take their barmitzvahs very seriously. Did Linda say anything about the lunch? Her sister's having terrible trouble with the caterers."

Holly didn't answer.

"Holly?"

"What?" snapped Holly in an irritated voice.

"All right, no need to bite my head off," said Mum with a surprised look. "I don't know what's got into you tonight. Linda said they have a big lunch after synagogue and then the kids have a party in the evening. Costs a fortune. What did Noah say about it?"

Holly sighed and dragged her eyes up from the screen, fingers poised. "He has to make a speech and he's dreading it and those horrible brothers of his..."

"...the twins or Gideon?"

"Gideon's OK but the twins are gross. They teased Noah and said he'd make a mess of it. You know he cries all the time?" She rolled her eyes.

Mum gave Holly a hard stare. "Linda's quite worried about Noah," she said.

Holly shrugged. She'd never spoken to Noah before Amy disappeared.

"She thinks he's being bullied at school," Mum went on. "So I said you'd keep an eye out for him, OK?"

Holly's phone pinged over and over. She pushed her chair back and stood up. "Yep. If you say so. Better go up, getting late."

She turned to go but Mum came round the table and laid a hand on her arm.

It felt so warm and gentle, Holly stopped. It was a long time since Mum had hugged her.

Probably because I'm fourteen now, she told herself.

"I know you're missing Amy, darling," Mum started.

Holly's phone pinged twice.

"You'll make a new best friend soon and for now, I'm just asking you to be kind to Noah. You've always been such a kind girl."

Holly's phone pinged.

"Sounds like you have some new friends already," said Mum and Holly could see she wanted to settle down with a cup of tea and hear all about it.

No way, Holly thought and shook herself free. "Um… yep… sure… OK. Night then."

Ignoring the puzzled look on Mum's face, she sprinted off upstairs, her feet as light as if they were gliding on air and going into her bedroom, she closed the door and threw herself onto the bed.

I'm all yours, Jay, she thought, a warm feeling spreading through her.

jay: U still there??
holly: yep mum came in
jay: mine not home for hours
holly: its 10.30
jay: shes partying
holly: wow

They messaged until after midnight. Holly's eyes were almost closing.

jay: U sleepy
holly: a bit
jay: ok chat later
holly: yep night jay
jay: nighty night

Holly woke with a start. Her clock said 3:10 and outside her window the sky was dark and clear. She could see a couple of stars shining.

Her phone was pinging and pinging. She picked it up and stared at the screen, rubbing sleep from her eyes.

jay: U awake ?? cant sleep
holly: yep im here
jay: cool so lonely here
holly: omg UR mum not home
jay: nope
holly: that's horrible
        : mine came back at ten
        : that was late
        : get scared home alone sometimes
jay: snap im not brave like some boys
holly: im here *smily emoji*
jay: sorry if i woke U
    : no one else to talk 2

jay is typing...

jay: thinking of mike
holly: so sorry maybe cos U told me
jay: think so
holly: dont wanna make U sad

jay: no way U make me feel happy holly
   :*laughing emoji*
holly: U can talk 2 me about anything
     : glad U woke me
jay: never met a girl like U lucky me
holly: *smily emoji*
       : amy never messaged like this
jay: all night??
holly: LOL we had sleepovers but not the same
jay: not on a school night
   : but can message any time
holly: yep and say anything
jay: anything at all

She had no idea what time she finally fell asleep. Then Mum was coming in with a cup of tea.

"Wake up, sleepy head," said Mum.

Holly's phone pinged twice as she pushed her hair out of her eyes and smiled to herself. That was Jay, she was pretty sure. She could hardly wait for Mum to leave the room to grab her phone and read the messages that streamed down the screen.

Jay's in my life now. I'm not alone anymore, she told herself.

Chapter 6
Most Wonderful Day

Holly walked all the way to school messaging Jay. She bumped into a lamppost and even stepped in front of a bus, leaping backwards just in time. She'd seen Madison and the other girls walking along tapping their phones like this. They were always giggling over photos and messages from boys, comparing notes and teasing each other.

I feel just like them now, she told herself.

Was it really only last night she and Jay had hooked up? They'd exchanged over fifty messages already – the number sent a thrill down her spine. WOW! as Jay would say. Jay's a good friend, she thought.

As good as Amy? she wondered. Perhaps not yet but he's so kind and sweet and he's been through so much what with his dad disappearing and his best friend being killed and his mum out all night. He's just as scared as me home alone. Wouldn't think boys were like that.

As she crossed the road she glanced up from her phone and saw Noah up ahead, his back against a wall.

Rick Gold was jabbing a finger at his chest, growling at him, "...so keep your mouth shut, you idiot!"

Noah's face was screwed up in a scared look. Rick gave him a final push and strode off towards school.

Holly looked around but no-one seemed to have noticed. Is this what Mum meant when she said Noah was being bullied? She gave an inward sigh. I don't have time for this. Me and Jay need to chat before school starts.

Her phone pinged in her hand but then Noah looked over and caught her eye. His face was wet with tears. He swiped away at them with the back of his hand.

Holly walked up to him. "All right?" she said. "What did Rick want?"

Noah shook his head. "Can't say," he muttered.

Who cares? thought Holly.

But then she remembered Mum asking her to look out for Noah. With an irritated sigh she said, "Oh, come on."

Noah shuffled along beside her. "We used to be good friends," he said.

"You and Rick?" That's a surprise, thought Holly. What have they got in common?

"We're in the same synagogue."

"The one where your cousin's having his barmitzvah?"

Noah nodded. "We always played together when we were little, even went back to each other's houses sometimes after religion class on Sundays."

"What happened?" Holly couldn't help asking, even though she didn't care that much. Not even about Rick anymore since Jay.

"We did something so stupid and now..."

They were walking alongside the basketball court and a boy shouted, "There he is, cry baby Levy."

Holly turned to see someone pointing towards Noah, Rick standing nearby, hands shoved in his pockets.

Noah stopped in his tracks, clutching the straps of his rucksack.

Holly felt a wave of irritation go through her. She grabbed Noah's arm and steered him towards a side door. "Ignore them, they're not worth it," she said, tossing her hair. Pushing open the door, she led the way into school.

"Thanks, Holly," muttered Noah.

She glanced down at him from her extra centimetres. It made her feel quite grown up, taking charge like that.

"S'OK," she said.

Then her phone pinged twice.

"You have to turn it off inside," said Noah, nodding to her phone.

Holly creased up her face and curled her lip. "Do you always do what you're told?"

Noah shrugged. "Mostly."

"Yeah, well, I'm busy."

She watched as Noah wandered off. Then going into an empty classroom, she sat down away from the door.

jay: can we talk??

holly: yep 10 mins to bell

jay: anyone there??

holly: no one but i saved a boy from bullies

jay: cool UR such a nice girl

   : was he a nice boy?

holly: LOL no

jay : U saved a nasty boy?

holly: no just a boring weepy boy
jay: like me???
holly: OMG nothing like U jay UR not boring
jay: and i dont cry
    : promise

Holly grinned. This was the absolute best way to start the day. They messaged for another five minutes and then she said she had to go.

holly: catch up at lunch double maths now
jay: me 2!!! *annoyed emoji*
holly: *girl waving emoji*

By third lesson, just before lunch, Holly had perfected the art of checking her phone without a teacher catching her. It was easy really. Keep the phone on silent. Cradle it in her lap under the desk. Lean slightly back in the chair, pen over notebook, head bent over her work. Glance at the screen for no more than 2 seconds at a time.

Coming up for air she caught Madison's eye. Madison gave her a long slow wink and nodded towards Holly's lap.

Yes! thought Holly. Boyfriend, she wanted to mouth to Madison but thought better of it as Madison turned back to her work.

As soon as the lunch bell went, Holly skipped out ahead of the crowd to the dining room, grabbed a sandwich, paid for it in record time and then took herself outside to a quiet bench. Settling down with a happy sigh she thought, Now it's just me and Jay.

jay: come on holly!! been waiting ages
holly: sorry how was maths?
jay: same old U?
holly: bad homework marks dont get algebra
jay: noooo!!! me 2!! hate algebra
holly: and PE
jay : hate PE
holly: but i like everything else
    : dont have a fave subject U?
jay: UR just like me
   : exactly the same
   : *sticker, boy saying FOR REAL*

Holly grinned but then she hesitated, fingers poised. Should she tell him she liked homework? Would he think she was boring? Not yet, she decided.

jay: U still there??
holly: yep i collect stuff
jay: wow
holly: old stuff like small things
    : teaspoons bits of jewellery tiny boxes
jay: cant believe it!!
   : i collect old stuff too
holly: u like vintage shops??
jay: LUV vintage shops!! we have millions in our town

Should she tell him she goes to North Laines? He could be in Brighton, couldn't he? He knows a lot of people I know, she told herself. But Aisha's warning voice was still in her head. Not yet, she thought.

holly: we have some too
jay: where
holly: around
jay: ok

There was a pause and Holly wondered if she'd offended him. She stared at the screen, breath held, hoping he wouldn't just disappear.

jay is typing...

Holly let her breath out with relief.

jay: we don't know each other that well yet
    : *sticker; boy, hand raised saying HIGH FIVE*
holly: LOL

As her phone pinged she heard Madison say, "Get you Holly Bennett, on your phone all lunch time now!"

Holly looked up to see Madison and the Bezzies staring down at her. Aisha was frowning a bit but when wasn't she? thought Holly, tossing her hair back.

"Anything you want to tell us?" asked Madison, flashing a knowing grin round the other girls.

They tittered back.

Holly went red and stammered, "N... n... no Madison, just wanted some fresh air."

"Oh yes?" said Madison, her voice rising up in disbelief but there was a kind smile on her face. "Well, I'm a very good listener, Holly sweetie, so just let me know if you need to chat."

Holly went even more red if that was possible and

nodded. The girls glided away to their favourite bench.

As she watched them go she saw Ellen hovering in a doorway looking behind her and then Tim appeared. They fell into step together, heads bent, chattering away like long lost friends.

They can't be talking about those stupid puppies the whole time, she thought and wondered if they'd had lunch together. Was Ellen still stuffing down chips, the buttons on her shirt almost popping off? Did Tim still cough before he dared to open his mouth?

Her phone was pinging and she stared at her screen. I've got Jay now in school as well as at home, she told herself, grinning at the latest messages.

Before she knew it break was over and she was back in Science with the computer games boys. She ploughed through experiment after experiment, rerunning Jay's messages through her head. Once she even laughed aloud and the games boys stared at her as if she was mad.

She poked her tongue out at them and their eyes widened until she thought they would pop out like Ellen's buttons.

Who cares what they think of me? she thought. Jay thinks I'm a nice girl.

A message from Mum came in before the end of school.

Going over to Gran's. Dad back tonight by six so you can have dinner together. Promise we'll shop on Saturday for that jacket xxx Mum

Holly was almost disappointed Dad would be home

early for once. She'd much rather spend the evening with Jay now.

Hopefully Dad will be tired, she told herself as she walked out of school, eyes glued to the screen. I'll get stuff out the freezer for dinner, we can eat quickly and then I'll say the magic word – homework. Dad'll want us to watch our fave crime thriller together, of course, but not tonight, she thought. I'm busy.

Holly felt a bit of a pang remembering Thursday nights curled up in her favourite armchair, Mum and Dad on the sofa and a box of chocolates open on the coffee table. In the weeks after Amy left when life felt so lonely and Amy didn't seem to have time even to message her, Thursday nights were about the only thing to look forward to in the week.

But Amy sent messages every day now, including this afternoon; photos with Gabe and her new crowd. She didn't ask anything about Holly.

She thinks she knows me, Holly told herself, as she arrived home and let herself in. She has no idea, has she?

The phone pinged as she dumped her stuff and ran upstairs to change. She chose her nicest top. Want to look my best for Jay, she told herself, checking her hair in the mirror.

Then she went back downstairs and straight to the kitchen.

I don't mind being home alone, anymore, she thought but as she grabbed her phone, there was another pic from Amy with her sleepover crowd.

She's really rubbing my face in her brand-new life, she thought, an angry feeling creeping through her.

Her phone pinged again. It was Jay.

jay: how was school?
holly: good
jay: yep?
holly: well

She hesitated. Can I tell him anything? she wondered, her fingers poised over the screen. Can I trust Jay? Amy added him too. If I say what I'm feeling right now about Amy, will Jay go and tell her?

She and Jay were already using Direct Messaging so their chats were private but still; he could say something to Amy, couldn't he?

jay: what? U can trust me holly
     : wont tell anyone
     : we R private!!!

Relief flooded her. He gets me, he really does, she told herself, her fingers tapping away.

holly: amy keeps sending me pics of her and gabe
     : her boyfriend
jay: oh
holly: pics of her and her crowd having sleepovers
     : looks so much fun
jay: harsh
holly: yep

holly is typing...
holly: me n amy never had a crowd.
     : did everything together

jay: i so get it holly
　　: me n mike were the same
holly: yep
　　: only
jay: go on im listening
holly: amy doesnt get it
　　: shes making me feel so bad
　　: im all alone an shes got a whole new life
jay: sort of rubbing ur face in it
holly: yep
jay: *emoji, face with downturned mouth*
holly: dont understand her anymore
jay: so sorry UR hurting
　　: she should think about UR feelings
　　: maybe amy isnt friend U thought
　　: shes a meangirl if U ask me!!

Holly stared at the screen, not sure what to think.
Jay was leaping to her defence and that was so sweet. It
was really nice to have someone to pour out her feelings
to. But Amy mean? That didn't feel right.

jay: RUOK
holly: amy was the best friend i ever had
jay: yeah course
　　: i get it holly
　　: sorry if i was harsh
　　: im here 4 U
　　: i wont let U down promise
holly: yep good
　　: thats ok
jay: phew!!

: still friends?
holly: *emoji, grinning face*
    : yep course

It was quite dark outside when she looked up from the screen. The kitchen clock said 6:10. Holly went over to the freezer, pulled out two pizzas and put them in the oven and switched on. They'd be ready in fifteen minutes and Dad was due home.

Then her phone pinged. It was a text from Dad.

Car broken down. Stuck on motorway. Wont get home for dinner. Sorry Hol Pol. xx Dad.

Home alone again, Holly thought and she glanced over her shoulder at a loud creak. She'd give anything to be able to run over to Amy's now. The house felt so empty. Amy would give her a big hug. Her mum would probably hug her too.

No-one hugs me these days, she thought and a chill went through her.

Her phone pinged.

jay: what RU doing??
holly: nothing no one home again
    : *two sad faces*
jay: * sticker, boy saying, I KNOW HOW YOU FEEL*
holly: pizza again
jay: snap, pizza three nights this week
    : HEY!!! dinner together??
    : pop a couple of cans?

Holly laughed out loud. Dinner with Jay. That was just what she needed. She threw herself to her feet and did a twirl. Who cares about creaks and shadows? "Not me when I'm with Jay," she said out loud.

They messaged until the early hours. Holly heard Mum come in around ten and even put her head round the bedroom door but Holly pretended to be asleep.

All she could think about was Jay. She fell asleep clutching her phone and woke up with Jay's messages dancing before her eyes.

Yesterday was the most wonderful day of my life, she told herself, stretching in bed with a smile on her face. And now we've got all day today together.

Life couldn't get any better.

Chapter 7
Confiscated

There was a smell of frying as Holly went down to breakfast next morning, her mind full of Jay. I'll go to school a bit early, she thought, and we can message before class.

In the kitchen Mum was dishing up eggs and bacon onto a line of plates on the counter.

Dad was sitting at the table buttering toast, his Coolest Dad in the Street mug Holly had given him last Father's Day, steaming with black coffee.

"Good morning, Hol Pol," Dad said, his comfortable grin spreading over his face. "Mum's cooking up a storm. She's feeling guilty."

"What? No I'm not," said Mum, over her shoulder as Holly sat down. "Well just a bit maybe." Strands of hair were stuck to her forehead and her face was red from the heat of the cooker. She wiped a tea towel over her face and flicked it at Dad.

Dad rolled his eyes at Holly.

"No-one's had much home cooking lately, what with

Gran's knee and everything," said Mum, cracking two more eggs.

"S'OK," said Holly. Her phone pinged twice.

"Popular girl," said Dad. "Not much time for home cooking, eh Hol?"

Holly threw him a scornful look. Her phone pinged again.

Mum passed over the breakfast plates and sat down, saying, "Phones silent or off at the table please, darling. You know the rules."

"Mu-um!" said Holly but she put her phone to silent.

"What a week!" Mum went on. "Gran's gone from bad to worse and poor Holly's been looking after herself every evening, haven't you darling?"

"She's a superstar," said Dad, cutting into his bacon.

Holly shrugged.

"So, tonight I'm cooking a special dinner and we'll sit down together as a family. Gran says she's feeling much better and wants some 'alone' time." Mum gave a little shake of her head.

"Sounds good to me," said Dad, grinning and pointing his knife towards Holly.

"Who cares?" said Holly with another shrug.

Dad gave her a puzzled look.

Holly dropped her eyes back to the screen but she felt herself go red. It was one of their 'things'; rolling their eyes and laughing at Mum. Dad was more laid back than Mum who liked to plan every moment, usually for the entire year ahead.

Dad would say, 'Let's see what today brings, worry about tomorrow when it comes,' and he and Holly would roll their eyes.

But he just doesn't get it, she thought now. Even if I told him about Jay – which I absolutely don't want to do yet – he wouldn't understand. I'm not his little girl anymore, sharing all his lame jokes.

Mum was still rattling away, "…and tomorrow morning we'll go shopping, get that new jacket."

Holly tapped the screen and grinned. Jay was sending streams of emojis.

"Holly?" Mum's voice was rising.

"Mmmm," she murmured.

"Honestly, you're stuck to that screen all the time, now," grumbled Mum.

"Nice she's making new friends," said Dad in a meaningful tone.

Out of the corner of her eye, Holly saw him crease his eyebrows at Mum. "Since, you know, Amy left," he went on in a low tone.

"Oh, yes, well, I suppose so," said Mum. "That phone never stops pinging these days. And you're fine by yourself now, darling? When I have to be with Gran?"

Holly didn't answer.

"Holly? I said you're fine by yourself for a couple of hours? Earth to Holly… honestly, it's like talking to a brick wall."

Holly looked up from her phone, eyes glazed over. Jay had just told her the anniversary of Mike's death was coming up.

jay : next week 1 year since mike died

"Holly?" Mum was looking very annoyed.

"Just a sec," she snapped, eyes back on the screen, tapping away.

holly: so sorry jay
jay: cant believe it
holly: must be unreal
jay: yep
   : no one 2 talk 2
holly: U can talk to me
jay : yes!!! UR the best girl ever!!!!

"I don't know what's got into you today," said Mum, her tone rising again. "Family dinner, tonight. I'm making your favourite. Or are you too busy?"

"Whatever," said Holly, looking up and then back to the screen.

Who cares what Mum and Dad are doing when Jay needs me? she thought.

"Enough of the whatever," grumbled Mum, "time you put that phone down and actually communicated with your family at the table."

She threw Dad a meaningful look, but Holly could see he wasn't listening anymore as he flicked through some work papers.

I'm out of here, she decided, and pushing back her chair, she said, "Laters."

Before Mum could nag her about anything else, she was down the hallway, grabbing her coat and school bag and out of the front door.

It was a dry, cold Friday morning and a fresh smell of the sea drifted up from the beach. Almost the weekend, she told herself and then me and Jay can message without school getting in the way for once.

He's really going to need me this week with Mike's anniversary coming up, she thought. Although she felt sorry, secretly she was pleased to be needed.

cant imagine going through this without U holly Jay had messaged earlier.

U dont have 2 she'd sent back.

Have I really only known him for less than two days, just since Wednesday evening?

It felt like weeks already. I know so much about him, she told herself, taking her eyes off the screen long enough to cross the road.

Buses were trundling down the main road between Brighton and Hove and seagulls were wheeling overhead. A huge bird landed on the overflowing rubbish bin at the crossing and she saw it peck away at some stale chips.

Maybe me and Jay can have fish and chips on the beach one day, she thought. On my favourite part of the beach, under the pier. She loved the rusty old iron girders and the wooden walkway of the pier stretching above her. It was like her secret place.

When she and Amy were little they used to pretend they lived under the pier, taking an old blanket and laying out crisps and cola cans as if they were having dinner. Their parents would be sitting on deckchairs sunning themselves, far enough away so that they couldn't hear anything.

"No-one knows where we are," Amy would say. "We're on a desert island."

"And we've been ship wrecked," added Holly, "so we can't get home."

That was how Holly liked it best, playing with Amy, just the two of them.

Amy had a big brother and lots of cousins. Sometimes they all gathered for family tea on Sunday afternoons. Holly was usually invited but not if tea was at someone else's house. Then she sat staring out of the living room window, waiting for Amy to come home.

Amy always came over to hers when she returned, full of stories about Aunty Sal who loved Bake Off and had made a crazy cake or Cousin Will who'd fallen out of his treehouse and broken *both* arms.

Holly would have to be patient and wait until Amy had run out of family news before she could suggest a game or something.

We were never bored with each other, she told herself now. Before Jay, I didn't need anyone else. But I can talk to Jay about anything, it's like we're old friends. I've told him loads of stuff about me and Amy and school and my family. He knows all about Gran's Crisis – although he did message, lucky me: i get more time with U.

He wasn't being mean or anything about Gran; she felt the same way and of course she loved Gran and didn't want her to have problems or anything. But now that Mum and Dad were always out, she and Jay had so much extra time to get to know each other. It was amazing how much they had in common.

As Holly neared the school gates, the pavement started to fill up with other kids but she just glided round them, fingers tapping, eyes glued to the screen.

There were only a few minutes before the bell but as she made her way through a side door, hoping for a last minute alone with Jay, a voice called down the corridor, "Holly Bennett, phone confiscated!"

Holly looked up in horror.

Miss Holland, the PE teacher, was striding towards her in a navy tracksuit, long hair pulled back in a scrunchy, right hand outstretched.

"Oh no, please Miss Holland. I was just turning it off," blurted out Holly, thrusting her phone into her bag.

"You know the rules. No phones in school." Miss Holland clicked her fingers.

It was no use. Holly pulled out the phone glancing at the screen alive with Jay's messages, switched it off and laid it in the teacher's hand.

"First offence?"

"Oh yes, Miss," said Holly in a breathless voice, fingers crossed behind her back.

The teacher paused, foot tapping, looking down at Holly. "Come to me at three thirty to collect it. And make sure you behave yourself until then." She turned on her heel and marched off down the corridor.

"Yes Miss, thanks Miss," Holly called after her with relief.

Confiscation could mean all term so that was lucky in a way. Jay would find another girl wouldn't he? He was already friends with Amy and Becca and at least two other girls Holly knew. He was such a nice boy. It wouldn't take him long to find someone new.

The thought made her so miserable. Her only hope was that as they were both stuck in school all day he might not notice she wasn't messaging.

I'll make it up to him after school, she told herself.

Jay will understand. Bet it's even happened to him at least once.

Only six and a half hours to go. It's not that long and comforted by these thoughts, she went into class.

The morning really dragged for once without her phone. Madison caught her eye in History and nodded down at her lap. Holly shook her head and mouthed, *Confiscated*. Madison rolled her eyes and for a moment Holly felt quite cheered as though she'd achieved some sort of street cred. But then she felt miserable again, missing Jay's messages.

Finally it was lunchtime and she followed the others into the dining hall. Nothing to rush for today, she told herself and decided on a plate of chips and sausage for once. She didn't have to eat healthily all the time just because Mum said.

She paid, walked straight over to Ellen's table and dumped the tray. Before she sat down she noticed Noah wandering around looking for a seat. There was a place at their table but she didn't call him over. What if Ellen didn't like it? Where would she sit then?

Ellen was eating her usual plate of chips. She took one look at Holly's plate and opened her mouth as if to make one of her mean remarks. Then staring at Holly for a moment – which was weird – she closed her mouth again, nodded and shifted her plate slightly to make a bit more room.

What's that all about? thought Holly as she ripped open a ketchup sachet and smothered her chips.

"Your hair," began Ellen in her usual abrupt way. "You born like that?"

Holly was looking at her plate. Did she really want to eat all this? Then with a sigh she shifted her gaze to Ellen and said, "Course not. I straighten it."

"How?"

"Straighteners."

Ellen frowned and shook her head. "You what?"

Holly gave a sigh. "You know, electric straighteners. You buy them. In a shop."

"OK." Ellen was narrowing her eyes. Then with what seemed a supreme effort of self-control, she changed her look to a more friendly one and muttered, "My hair's always a mess."

Holly nodded. She wasn't going to disagree.

There was a pause as they both ate some chips, Ellen shovelling in twice as many as Holly.

Then Ellen said, "Could you do mine? You know, straighten it." Before Holly could answer, Ellen rushed on, "Only Tim's asked me up to his place tomorrow to see the puppies and… well… look at me." She glanced down and noticing one of her buttons had popped out, tried to squeeze it back into the button hole but failed and gave up with a sigh."

Holly stared at Ellen with renewed interest. "Oh," she said. "So you like him?"

Ellen shrugged and then fixed Holly with her blue eyes.

It was the first time they'd really stared at each other. It gave Holly a warm sort of feeling all over. Like they were friends. Nothing like that had happened for ages.

It reminded her how it felt to hang with Amy at school. Sometimes when they were out in the playground a couple of the other girls would drift over to join them, which was quite nice. Although Holly never really liked it when Becca Wilson joined them. It often felt to Holly that Becca wanted Amy all to herself, which made Holly feel worried although she never said anything to Amy.

Becca was one of those sharp-faced girls, with narrow hips and shoulders and hair which fell over her face, often hiding her eyes. She loved to keep on top of the gossip and whisper it behind her hand, usually in Amy's ear so Holly felt left out.

Becca hung around on the edge of Madison and the Bezzies and she seemed to know everyone. Since Amy had left, Holly only saw Becca in the distance or on her phone.

But it was Becca who'd done the Shoutout for Jay, she reminded herself. So that was a good thing.

Now Ellen was actually asking her for help and she couldn't help thinking it would be fun to have a friend over to talk about hair and clothes.

Maybe boyfriends, too.

"OK," she said with a brief nod. "Come over to mine around ten tomorrow. Just for an hour, have to go shopping later." Mum kept reminding her about buying that new jacket but she didn't like mentioning a mother to Ellen.

Ellen's shoulders drooped.

Now what? thought Holly, feeling irritated. What else am I supposed to say?

Then Ellen blurted out, "I've got nothing to wear. Since Mum... you know... passed... there's no-one to go shopping with and my Dad works all the time, evenings as well... he's really nice my Dad..." She paused and there was an awkward moment.

Holly felt herself go red. What if Mum died like Grandad did? shot through her mind. The thought was so awful her throat closed up and she dropped the chip she was holding back on the plate.

"But he's no good about clothes and eating healthy stuff." Ellen flicked her head at her plate.

Holly didn't know what to say but fortunately Ellen carried on talking, "Dad works two jobs since we lost Mum's wage. I'd be really lonely at home without my animals. I've got three cats; there's a fox I feed in the garden and then there's the squirrels. I don't really get the other girls…"

She narrowed her eyes at Holly as if expecting her to say something mean.

Holly kept quiet.

"Anyway," finished Ellen. "No point in going shopping. Nothing ever fits me." She stopped and picked up another chip, stared at it and then put it down again.

Well, we've got something in common, thought Holly. I don't really get the other girls either. Most of them want to be in Madison's crowd and those who don't, like Becca Wilson, ignore me now Amy's gone.

But a makeover for Ellen. Now that's a challenge.

"You don't need to change that much," she said.

Stylist Sandi's voice was in her head. Sandi was always saying, *Make the most of what you've got and be positive.*

"If you got some new uniform, you'd look great," Holly went on.

"Really?"

"Course. Get a new blouse and cardigan, maybe next size up and a skirt that doesn't grip your waist. But for tomorrow I've got a black jumper that would look good on you. Bring the black leggings we wear for PE"

Ellen nodded. "I could wear trainers, I suppose."

"Perfect," said Holly, flashing a grin. "I'll straighten your hair and lend you accessories…"

"…you what?"

"Trust me, Tim'll be blown away." Holly picked up her tray, the food hardly touched. "See you in the morning."

They swapped mobile numbers and Holly said she'd message Ellen her address later.

As she walked away from the table it felt like she was floating on air. Ellen had turned to her for help, not Madison or gossipy Becca. And it was only two and a half hours before she got her phone back and she could tell Jay all about her day.

She couldn't wait.

Chapter 8
Do You Really Care?

After school Holly raced round to the PE office to retrieve her phone. Miss Holland was telling off two girls for skipping PE. Her voice was loud enough to be heard as Holly waited out in the corridor, hopping from foot to foot until she thought she'd go mad.

Finally the girls slouched out complaining in loud voices about how much they hated school.

Holly peered round the door and said in a timid voice, "Miss Holland?"

The teacher looked up with a glare and then pulling open a desk drawer handed over the phone, saying, "Don't let me catch you again this term or you won't see that phone until after Easter."

"No Miss, thanks Miss," said Holly in her most grovelling voice.

As she walked away, hands trembling, she put the phone on and swiped. The corridor echoed with the sound of Jay's messages pinging and pinging. He'd been trying her all day.

The last message was the most heart rending.

jay: thought U cared about me??
  : did i get U wrong holly????

Her eyes were almost blurred with tears as she tapped back,

holly: SOOO SORRY JAY!!!! PHONE CONFISCATED ALL
    DAY!!!
  : i do care
  : really really really care

There was no reply. Jay wasn't even typing. With trembling fingers she sent another message.

holly: will NEVER NEVER happen again!!! PROMISE!!!

Still no messages from Jay as she walked out of school and along the road past the bus queue, everyone shouting and pushing and throwing bags around.

Why hasn't he replied? she thought, numb with worry.

Becca was at the end of the queue and without meaning to Holly caught her eye. Becca smirked, her hair falling around her face and then whispered something behind her hand to another girl.

What does that mean? thought Holly. Has Jay messaged her because I wasn't around today?

A cold feeling crept up through her. What if Jay's moved on to Becca? Dumped me?

Her phone pinged.

jay: was it really confiscated???
holly: course wouldn't lie to U
jay: long day without U
holly: same
     : HORRIBLE DAY!!
jay : no one 2 talk 2
holly: sooo lonely

She felt a bit mean saying this because she'd enjoyed hanging with Ellen at lunchtime and was looking forward to their makeover session on Saturday morning.

That's girl stuff, she told herself. Boys aren't interested in all that.

jay : thought U dumped me
   : bored with me
holly: NO!!!! NEVER!!!
   : really really like talking to U
jay : U dont have 2 pretend
holly: im not
     : honest !!
     : want to talk n talk n talk

No messages came back for so long Holly told herself, it's over. I've blown it and now I'm all alone again. She walked for another five minutes and was nearly home.

Then her phone pinged.

jay: so there isnt another boy??
holly: absolutely definitely honestly NOT!!
jay: RU sure??
holly: YES!!!

    : been miserable all day

jay: me 2 didnt know what to do

holly: me 2

    : so worried about U

    : mikes anniversary coming up

jay: been getting me down all day

holly: sooo sorry jay

    : poor U

jay is typing...

jay: *sticker: boy smiling surrounded by hearts saying

    YOU'RE THE SWEETEST*

Holly stared at her phone, her legs weak with relief. He's forgiven me. She almost couldn't believe it.

Three more cartoon stickers came over in quick succession; MISSED YA/U GET ME. The third one was a sticker of a boy with a rainbow over his head.

Holly gave a happy sigh.

holly: luv the rainbow!!!

jay: how U make me feel

holly: really glad

jay: yep me 2

    : sorry ur phone taken!!

    : bummer!!!!

holly: real bummer

jay: so we good???

holly: oh yes

    : 150% good

jay: *smiling emojis*
holly: *smiling emoji*
    : home now and mum here
jay : laters babe

OMG! He called me babe, thought Holly, Her heart felt as if it would burst.

As she let herself in through the front door and dumped her bag in the hall, she could feel her cheeks flaming. But not because I'm upset for once, she thought. It was sheer joy.

"Good day at school?" said Mum, as she went into the kitchen.

Holly opened the fridge and took out a yoghurt. "The best," she said and grabbed a spoon from the open dishwasher.

"Hey, that's dirty! Haven't run it yet," called out Mum. "Daydreamer." She gave a laugh and checked the oven. "Dinner at six. Dad home early today."

Holly was already walking out of the door. As she floated upstairs to her room and threw herself on the bed, she thought, Everything's changed since Wednesday. I've met a boy; I don't mind being home alone so much anymore; I sent Gran a huge Get Well card and it's the weekend! No miserable teachers on my back to confiscate my phone for two whole days.

She switched on her straighteners and changed out of her uniform while they heated up. She chose leggings and her tightest fitting top and then sat in front of the mirror working on her hair until it was gleaming and straight as a ruler. She tried out different smiles – for Jay, she told herself – and then with her mouth open she ran her tongue slowly over her top lip. It felt weird and if she was honest, a bit sexy.

She'd seen Madison do that a couple of days ago when she was telling the Bezzies and anyone who cared to listen – like me, thought Holly – about a row she'd had with Harry.

"So he was nearly ten minutes late for our third date," Madison told them. "You can imagine how furious I was and when he *finally* showed up," her hands were on her hips at this point, chin shoved forward, "he didn't even say sorry."

Gasps from the other girls.

Madison raised her eyebrows and tilted her head. "So we had this massive row," she went on, "and I told him we're finished."

"OMG Madison, what did he say?" asked a girl in a breathless voice.

"He begged me to take him back and I wouldn't."

"I would've done the same," said Aisha.

Holly was sure she looked a tiny bit bored. Probably heard all this before, she told herself. Madison always expected the Bezzies to listen to repeat versions of her stories.

Madison looked round the group, making them wait. Then she said, "But then I took him back, didn't I?"

The admiring crowd cooed and sighed.

"He kissed me about a million times," she went on. "Making up's the best bit about rowing. Harry's an awesome kisser." Then she opened her mouth and ran her tongue slowly over her top lip.

Now as Holly stared at herself in the mirror, her tongue sort of stuck on a dry bit at the corner of her mouth she thought, Wonder if Jay's a great kisser. How would I know? I've never kissed a boy.

Her phone pinged. It was a message from Amy, another picture of her and Gabe.

She wanted to message back: is gabe a good kisser?

As far as she knew, Amy had never kissed a boy before Canada. But maybe everyone does it over there and maybe Amy's kissed loads of boys now.

As her fingers hovered over the keypad, she thought, No, I don't want to tell Amy about Jay. Not yet.

Mum called her down to dinner and when Holly went into the kitchen, Dad was sitting at the table, jacket off, tie loose, sleeves rolled up.

"You look nice, Hol Pol," said Dad, his eyes wide. "Off out tonight?"

Holly blushed and dropped her head. "No," she mumbled.

"So just for your old dad, hey?" He rolled his eyes.

Holly shrugged.

She sat down as Mum crashed a couple of pans in the sink and pulled open the oven door. There was a huge chicken crackling in the heat, surrounded by crisp roast potatoes. Holly felt her stomach rumble.

"You've cooked up a storm tonight, darling," called out Dad and he picked up the carving knife. "Bring it on."

Holly put her phone on silent and felt herself relax. They were going to have a nice family meal; a bit like old times, she thought, except I might have invited Amy before Canada. There was a pang but she gave an inward shrug. Who cares about Amy? She doesn't care about me.

I'll make some excuse after dinner, she told herself, give the Friday night TV quiz a miss and go upstairs to my lovely Jay.

"Breast or leg?" asked Mum.

"Breast please," said Holly with a grin, "and loads of potatoes."

Mum dished up and Holly helped herself to broccoli and carrots, pouring thick gravy over the whole plate.

"Careful of your top," warned Mum as they all started to eat. "It'll show every little spot."

Holly nodded, her mouth full and Dad gave a snort.

They were quiet for a while but as the plates began to empty Mum said, "So in the morning Holly, I've got Salsa until midday in town. Meet me at Churchill Square just after twelve to get that new jacket. Do your homework in the morning so you don't leave it all weekend."

Holly rolled her eyes at Dad and the broad grin he gave her made her want to cheer. She hadn't realised how much she'd missed the three of them sitting together. Maybe Gran's Crisis was over and they could get back to normal.

She went off into a daydream about meeting Jay – what does he even look like? – and then inviting him home to meet Mum and Dad. He could come on a Friday evening and they could snuggle together on the sofa afterwards and watched the TV quiz, their fave family programme.

She was snapped out of her thoughts by Mum saying, "Holly? Are you listening? I said I want you to make sure you've finished all your homework before Sunday because we're going to Gran's for the whole day. All three of us."

What! thought Holly. When am I going to have time with Jay? Is she mad?

A spear of anger ripped up through her and before she knew it she was yelling, "Who says you can fill up every single minute of my life! Homework Saturday, Gran Sunday. When am I supposed to have time for myself! I'm fourteen, not a little kid!"

Pushing back her chair so hard it tipped over with a crash, she threw herself to her feet, eyes flashing.

"Steady on, Hol Pol," said Dad. "Your Mum was only…"

"Whatever!"

As she stormed out of the kitchen Mum's voice echoed down the hall behind her. "Come right back here, young lady. What on earth has got into you?"

But Holly raced up the stairs two at a time, went into her bedroom and slammed the door behind her as hard as she could. The whole house seemed to rattle around her.

As she threw herself down at the table and caught her face in the mirror, it was as though she was staring at a stranger. Her hair was all messy, sticking out in places and her skin was blotchy from shouting.

But it was her eyes which held her gaze the most. She'd never seen them so wild. It was a bit scary, she had to admit. She'd never really shouted at her parents like that before. She'd always been good little Holly, playing with Amy and behaving herself at school.

Well I've changed, she thought, sticking her lower lip out in defiance. It's not that I don't care about Gran – of course I do – but Mum and Dad just don't get me.

I'm not their little girl anymore.

I'm Jay's.

She raised her arm and placing her lips on the skin, she kissed herself.

Practising, she thought, for when I kiss Jay.

There was a little knock at the door and before she could answer, it opened and Dad was standing there, hands in his pockets.

"What just happened, Holly?" he said.

Holly shrugged. "Nothing."

"Hmm. Not seen you like that before."

"Mum doesn't understand. I'm fourteen, not four."

"Yes, true. Well, all right darling. But if there's anything else going on you want to talk to us abou…"

"…there isn't."

"If you're lonely or not making friends, missing Amy," Dad said.

Holly gave a snort. "Amy's gone and I'm not lonely. A friend's coming over in the morning to do homework together if you must know."

"Oh good. Well, be kind to your Mum, she's trying her best. Make an effort for me. Eh?"

Holly shrugged. "If you say so."

Dad's face fell a bit and Holly couldn't help feeling guilty. Her Mum and Dad were OK, much better than most and at least Mum wasn't dead like Ellen's Mum. She shuddered at the thought. But they have to understand I have my own life.

As Dad went outside she heard him say to Mum, "She's OK, don't worry. Probably just needs a bit of space. You know, teenage girls."

She couldn't hear Mum say anything back but for a second she thought she heard a sob. Mum crying? But then she heard them walk away downstairs, murmuring to each other.

All good, she told herself. I was right to get mad. Now perhaps they'll give me some privacy.

Chapter 9
Ellen

Holly lay in bed and watched the winter sunlight build behind the curtains. Her phone was completely dead after messaging with Jay for hours last night. She'd forgotten to put it on charge before she fell asleep.

Mum and Dad were out as usual; Dad meeting a client and Mum at Salsa class. But instead of lying in bed holding her breath like last Saturday morning and all the weeks before, since the beginning of Gran's Crisis, Holly stretched luxuriously.

She glanced at her bedside clock. Nearly ten. Ellen would be here soon.

Must get up and shower, she thought and throwing back the duvet, she jumped out of bed. Then she plugged her phone in to charge, grabbed her straighteners and plugged them in too.

After she was showered and dressed, she looked through her wardrobe pulling out a large black sweater with sparkly stripes around the cuffs and neck. She found some earrings she hadn't worn yet and some other bits.

Sandi's voice was in her head. *You don't have to have everything matching – like your mum. But they have to go together in some way. Like star earrings and a half moon necklace.*

Sandi always had such good advice. Holly wondered if Amy still looked at Sandi's YouTube channel. Maybe she didn't need it anymore now she had Gabe.

The doorbell rang; a single ding dong and Holly ran downstairs. It would be Ellen, she was sure. But I'll still check, she told herself, to be certain.

Sunlight was pouring through the glass panel as Holly peered out. Ellen's broad outline and frizzy hair was unmistakeable.

She threw open the front door with a smile on her face.

"Hi," said Ellen, throwing a glance over her shoulder. "This still OK?"

"Yep," said Holly. "Come in."

She led the way across the hall and upstairs to her bedroom.

"Nice," said Ellen, looking round as they went in. She stood in the doorway, hands in the pockets of her jacket. She was wearing black leggings, black jacket, trainers and a wool scarf around her neck.

Holly felt awkward too, so she said, "Do you have your own room?"

"Yeah, just me and Dad at home. Got three bedrooms. The spare room's Mum's sewing room."

"She made clothes?" said Holly.

"Dresses. She was good, always had loads of customers." Ellen rummaged in a bag hanging on one shoulder and handed Holly a photo.

Holly stared at the photo of a woman in her late thirties, quite short with a slender figure, small hands and feet and long red hair which fell in ringlets. "She's pretty," she said, handing the photo back.

Ellen's cheeks went pink and Holly could see she was pleased. "You have the same colour hair."

"Mum's was always so neat," said Ellen. "She looked after mine, did my plaits every morning until… God! I hate the way everyone at school goes on about hair and clothes."

Ellen had her ferocious voice on, eyes narrowing.

Holly gave a nervous laugh and said, "Yep, the fashion crowd."

"Fashion fascists," growled Ellen.

Holly flicked her hair back and glanced away. What if she turns mean and I'm on my own with her?

But Ellen seemed to sense she'd gone too far and said, "Who cares about Madison and that nasty Becca Wilson."

"Definitely," said Holly in a firm voice, although she didn't entirely agree about Madison. I sort of need her, don't I? she thought. Although maybe not so much anymore, not since Jay.

"OK, why don't you try this on," Holly pointed to the black jumper laid out on the bed.

Ellen stared at her for a few seconds and then lowered her eyes. "Change here?"

"Yeah, look, no fashion fascists here, right?" Holly put her hands up and grinned.

Ellen nodded and then pulled off the tatty cardigan she was wearing. She had a white polo shirt underneath and the collar was chewed up at each end.

"Who does your washing?" asked Holly.

"Me," growled Ellen. "Why?"

"Oh, well, of course," said Holly flustered. "It's just... I might give you some tips on washing your stuff so it doesn't get all messed up in the machine."

"Machine's broken. I go to the launderette."

"Oh."

"But Dad said he'd get a new one."

Holly threw her a relieved smile. "Right, that's something worth nagging for, trust me. If we're going for a whole new look then you need to take care of your clothes from now on, OK?"

Ellen stared at her for a moment, her blue eyes narrowed and then her face cleared and with a grin she said, "OK, let's do it."

Holly pulled a clean black T out of a drawer and insisted Ellen put it on under the black jumper. Once Ellen had changed Holly stood in front of her, tweaking and smoothing until she was satisfied. Then she offered the earrings and three silvery bangles. She had a moment of panic when she thought maybe Ellen didn't have pierced ears but although Ellen fumbled a bit – she had piercings but they'd started to close over – she managed to push in the earrings and then pulled on the bracelets. She had surprisingly slender wrists.

Holly grabbed one and said, "Hey, look. You have film star wrists. Mine are so, like, chubby." It was the kind of thing Sandi said.

Ellen blushed deep red and muttered, "Really?"

"Yep."

Then Holly pulled open her wardrobe door and turned Ellen to face the mirror. Ellen stared at herself and Holly could see she was pleased with the effect.

The other girl's legs looked longer in the leggings. The black jumper hung nicely down past her hips, sparkling at the wrists and neckline. Instead of plump, bursting-out-of-her-clothes Ellen, Holly saw a girl who looked about sixteen, with an interesting face and cool outfit. She felt a pang of jealousy.

"You look so much older," said Holly. "Like sixteen maybe seventeen."

Ellen shrugged but she looked a bit pleased with herself.

If I looked this grown up, thought Holly, Jay would love it.

She went off into a daydream about Jay when she felt a tapping on her arm.

"I said what about the hair or is it beyond help?" Ellen was fixing her with her blue eyes.

Holly shook herself. "Sorry. Sit down here," she pointed to a chair.

She felt Ellen's hair. She'd told her to wash it before she came. "Did you use conditioner?"

"Yeah, Mum had all that sort of stuff."

"Great."

Holly detangled the hair as far as she could with her fingers and then started with the straighteners. Fortunately Ellen's hair was quite fine. That made it easier and soon she felt like Sandi on YouTube, demonstrating a new look.

"So Tim," she said as she felt Ellen relax in the chair. "How long you known each other?"

"Just this term. We both like animals."

"Yes."

"Which you hate."

The straighteners wobbled in Holly's hand. "How did you know?"

"We could tell. Did you get bitten as a kid or something?"

Ellen was a well-behaved subject, sitting still and upright in her chair. Sandi would approve, thought Holly.

"My grandparents had a dog, Lucy…"

"…what breed?"

"Golden Labrador. We all loved her but Dad's allergic to animals and well, I find them scary. I mean, they all have teeth and claws, don't they?"

Ellen laughed. "Not really. It's about getting used to them. Come over to mine sometime and I'll show you. "

Holly nodded but she didn't think she would. Anyway, she thought, I don't have time with Jay and everything.

"Tim doesn't care about girls like Madison and her crowd," said Ellen, "going on about clothes and make-up all the time. And he doesn't treat me like I'm stupid or anything."

"That's good," said Holly, with a knowing nod. "Boys can be as bad as the fashion fascists."

"Tell me about it. And you?"

"Me what?" asked Holly, feeling how silky the hair was falling between her fingers.

"Got a boyfriend?"

There was a silence while Holly struggled to make her mind up. Should she, shouldn't she? But in the end she couldn't resist it. "Yep. Our age but not at our school."

"How did you meet?"

"Shoutout from Becca."

Ellen snorted. "Hate Becca Wilson. But I saw that message. Is he nice?"

"He's lovely."

"Live round here?"

"Not sure. Haven't actually met up yet. Still messaging."

Wouldn't it be nice to tell Amy about Jay, Holly couldn't help thinking. Amy had messaged a while ago saying how everyone at school loves her English accent and they all want to be her friend. Holly had been overwhelmed with jealousy. All she could think was, *I'm* Amy's best friend. Doesn't she remember?

Amy has never once said she misses me or even, why don't you come and visit me in Canada, she thought. Why should I even bother to tell her about my Jay?

Ellen was breaking into her thoughts. "Good to be wary but if he knows other people should be OK. What's his name?"

"Jay."

"Keep him away from Becca. She's such a gossip."

Holly felt a stab in her belly. "Oh?" Had Becca said something? But she didn't want to ask.

Ellen snorted again. "Becca's like, sooo dumb."

They laughed and Holly put the finishing touches to Ellen's hair.

"There. You look amazing. Tim will be smitten," said Holly, picking a couple of hairs off Ellen's sweater.

Ellen gave a little twirl, her red hair gleaming and quite straight now. "I feel so different."

"That's because of a more careful choice of clothes,"

said Holly in her Sandi voice but with a grin on her face. "Watch what you eat a bit more."

"Chips?"

Holly gave a nod. "Chips."

Ellen grinned and picked up her bag. "OK, better go. Meeting Tim at the bus stop. Thanks Holly. Appreciate it."

For a moment Holly thought Ellen was going to hug her and she felt a sort of longing go through her but the other girl ducked her head and said, "I'll see myself out."

Then she was gone and Holly heard her heavy tread on the stairs and the sound of the front door opening and closing again.

The silence settled back down around her. She gave a sigh as a leaden feeling swept through her.

But her next thought was, Jay!

Chapter 10
On the Beach

Holly put on her old jacket and a wool scarf. As she stepped outside the house, sunlight warmed her for the first time in weeks and there was a hint of spring in the air. Some of Mum's daffodils were beginning to bud and snowdrops were in full bloom around the pine tree in the middle of the front garden. She and Amy would have called this beach weather and headed off to the pier.

But I'm going to meet Jay, Holly thought as she walked to the bus stop, eyes glued to the screen. Her phone was fully charged now and as a precaution she'd put the charger in her bag. She had to meet Mum in an hour and she didn't want to run out of juice in the Mall.

jay: hey holly wassup?
holly: out for a walk
jay: great
holly: wanna come? *sun emoji*
jay: yep *smiley face*

The bus pulled up and Holly stepped on, swiped her pass and moved down the crowded aisle. It was peak time on Saturday morning and there was standing room only. Everyone was going to the shops and cafés in the middle of Brighton.

Students wearing T-shirts with Uni Rag Week across the front in dripping red letters, were shaking collection buckets. They had vampire teeth and fake blood smeared around their mouths.

It was always fun 'student watching' as she and Amy used to say. Especially at the weekends; the students were always doing something fun and usually completely crazy.

One very thin boy with shaved eyebrows and piercings through his lips and chin, rattled his bucket and called out, "Pay up folks or we'll suck your blood."

"Collecting beer money again?" sneered a man in paint-stained clothes, near the door.

The boy grinned and said, "Rag Week's charity this year is ChildrenFirst78. Good cause; they help kids keep safe online."

A wave of approval swept through the bus and the man dropped a pound coin into the bucket. The students cheered and other people gave money too.

Holly found a fifty pence piece in her purse and threw it in. The student with the piercings grinned again and nodding to her phone, said, "Watch your back, lot of rough people on the Web."

Holly nodded back. "We know all about that stuff from school."

"Awesome," said the boy.

The bus stopped at Churchill Square and all the students jumped off.

Holly stepped down too and walked towards the sea. It was a bit breezy now but still very sunny. A perfect morning to be with Jay in my favourite place, she thought. Under the pier. What if he asks me where I live today? Holly counted on her fingers from Wednesday. Only our fourth day. She had to admit the student on the bus had sent a spear of worry through her.

It's not that I don't trust Jay, she told herself. But we've got plenty of time to swap addresses and stuff. Jay will understand. He understands me better than Amy these days.

For the first time she wondered if she and Amy were still best friends and a hollow feeling rolled around inside her.

The crowds around the Mall were thinning out as she walked down the steep hill towards the beach and the coastal road.

Who cares about Amy? she thought, as she arrived at the traffic lights and pressed the button. Amy's gone to Canada.

The lights went red and Holly crossed over to the Promenade which ran all the way to Hove. There were kiosks selling candy floss, souvenirs and sweets and even in the winter lots of people were around, with kids on scooters and bikes.

Holly walked along until she reached a flight of steps which led down to the beach. The sea stretched before her in a great wide sweep to the horizon, more blue than grey in the sunlight this morning. The coastline of France was over seventy miles away and out of sight. In this part of the Channel there were no islands to break up the flat expanse of water.

Sometimes it felt a rather lonely view to Holly, like a great empty canvas waiting to be drawn on. Further round the coast to the west towards Portsmouth, the Isle of Wight with its low hills stretched across the horizon. After dark, lights twinkled along the island's silhouette. Holly always thought it would be nice to have something like that in the view out to sea from Brighton beach.

Today there was a long, rust red container boat moving slowly in the distance and windsurfers in wet suits bobbing around close to the beach. Quite busy for February, she thought.

The pier was over to her left and she could hear Beatles music pouring out of the speakers. A smell of chips in the air made her hungry but thinking of Ellen, she decided she'd wait until lunch with Mum.

She tipped back her face, enjoying the warmth from the sun. She couldn't help thinking back to last Saturday, waking up all alone with the delivery man banging on the door. It had felt then as if no-one cared about her anymore. Amy had her Canada crowd, Mum was running around after poor Gran and Dad was busy with his clients.

But then I met Jay, she told herself, and with a little smile on her face, she skipped down the steps to the pebbly beach. A few strides and she was under the pier. She made a little cushion with her scarf on the stones and settled down. A seagull landed just beyond her feet, pecking at a washed-up crab flipped on its back.

Waves were dragging back and forth over the pebbles making a delicious rushing sound. Amy used to say the sounds of the sea were their own personal playlist.

"We've heard it all our lives."

"Like our fave band," Holly would say and they'd giggle, their heads close together. She so missed being close to her friend.

Can't really snuggle up to Jay over my phone, she thought, but she couldn't help grinning.

What would Jay think of the sea? she wondered, as she breathed in the tangy smell of salt and seaweed, laced with chips. The best smell in the world, as she and Amy used to say.

They'd had a plan to bottle the smell and sell it in school. But no matter how hard they tried - emptying out water bottles and waving them about to trap that special scent – when they took the lid off at home there was a smell of nothing.

"The smell belongs to the sea," Amy said. "You can only find it at the beach."

A loud ping. Holly swiped her screen.

jay: RU there
holly: yep
    : luv saturday morning
    : sleep late
jay: yep me 2
holly: no homework
    : well not until later
jay: deserve a break
holly: haha try telling my mum that

holly is typing...

holly: today we R going shopping
    :tomorrow we have to go to gran ALL DAY!!
jay: bummer
   : do you have to help with shopping
holly: i need a new jacket
jay: OK *thumbs up emoji*
   : send me a pic when you get it
holly: OK

There was a pause and Holly heard laughter further along the beach. The students with the vampire teeth had arrived and were sitting around, swigging from beer bottles. A girl put on some music. Holly recognised the band and nodded her head in time to the beat.

Then one of the students yelled, "I'm going in."

The others started a slow hand clap as the boy pulled off his shoes and socks and then to Holly's amazement, his jeans – she could see he had black boxers on underneath, but still; she felt herself go red – and then he ran into the water, yelling at the cold.

"Freeeezing!!"

"You idiot!" called out the girl.

Someone pulled the girl's arm and she looked down, saying, "No… too cold… no… oh, shall I?"

More laughter and then suddenly the girl kicked off her pumps, pulled off *her* jeans and ran screaming into the waves.

Holly didn't know which way to look. Is that what you have to do when you go to uni? she wondered. What would Amy say? Or even Ellen? Should I tell Jay? But I'd have to say I was by the sea. Before she could make up her mind, her phone pinged.

jay: still there?
holly: yep
jay: inside or outside?
holly: oh, u know, around
jay: *emoji, turned down mouth*

Holly felt a pang of guilt. He thinks I'm mean, she thought.

Suddenly one of the students hollered in a deep voice, "Look out, mate!"

Holly swivelled her neck and the words of the boy on the bus came back to her... *lot of rough people on the web.*

The students were pushing each other about at the water's edge and getting soaked. She couldn't help grinning and then she tapped her phone.

holly: nice day so im outdoors
jay: cool me 2

jay is typing...

jay: wanted 2 ask u 4 a pic
    : heres mine

Jay's photo came on her phone. A boy about her age, with fair skin and light blond hair which flopped over his forehead, was looking straight at the camera. His eyes were a hazel colour and very wide, with long lashes. He had a broad grin on his rather narrow face and Holly felt he was smiling just for her. Dressed in a denim jacket, black jeans and Converse trainers, the boy – Jay, she told herself – was standing in a park and Holly could see some swings behind him and a football pitch in the distance.

He's gorgeous, she thought. Easily as gorgeous as Gabe – no – more so. He's absolutely perfect. She couldn't believe it as she stared and stared at the photo. My Jay.

Her phone pinged.

jay: *sticker: boy smiling, saying, CAN'T WAIT TO SEE YOU
   : dont keep me waiting

Holly stared at her phone for a minute and then she swiped through her pictures, looking for the right one. Jay kept on sending impatient messages as she rejected photo after photo. Finally she settled on one taken at New Year when her hair looked just right and she was wearing a nice top. Dad had taken it in the living room with the tree lit up in the background. There was a nice glow on her cheeks, which looked rosy instead of blotchy for once and she was smiling.

It'll have to do, she told herself, pressing Send.

jay is typing...

jay: LIKE WOW!!!
   : UR so beautiful
   : OMG
   : UR just awesome
holly: thanks ...blushing...
    : your pic is so nice jay
jay: no way
holly: way
jay: haha

holly: feel like turning somersaults

jay: had the same thought!!

holly: haha UR reading my mind

jay: OMG!! just thinking that

    : snap

holly: snap

jay: UR my girl beautiful holly

holly: UR my jay

jay: cant tell U how happy U make me

    : thinking about mike and his anniversary next week

holly: which day is it

jay: next saturday

    : maybe we

There was a pause and Holly waited. Maybe what? she wondered.

holly: U OK?

jay: yep

holly: maybe we could what?

jay: we could be together somehow

holly: for the anniversary

jay: yep

holly: course

    : we can message and stuff

jay: awesome

Holly glanced at the time on her phone. She was already late to meet Mum. Wish I didn't have to go, she thought. But I need that jacket and anyway, I'm already in Mum's bad books for slamming the door last night.

She stood up and brushed herself down.

holly: gotta go and meet mum
jay: OK
holly: rather keep messaging U
jay: *smiley emoji*
holly: wont be long
jay: promise???
holly: promise
jay: OK
  : xxx

He's sending me kisses!! thought Holly. Her fingers hovered over the keys and then she made her mind up.

holly: xxx

There! Done it, she thought. Her phone pinged.

jay: *sticker: boy with thoughtful face saying, U GET ME*

A warm feeling spread up through Holly as she dropped her phone in her jacket pocket and walked up the beach. There's no-one in the world like my Jay, she told herself. He's totally relying on me for support next Saturday for the anniversary of Mike's death, his Mum's useless – mine isn't but she doesn't get me, not like Jay – and he's sent me three kisses. She just wanted to stare and stare at Jay's photo but Mum was sending impatient messages.

mum: where are U?

: been waiting 20 minutes

: message me!!

holly: coming

Holly walked across the beach, up the steps and back over the road, quickening her pace as she approached Churchill Square. She spotted Mum near the bus stop in front of the Mall, scanning the crowds.

A peculiar feeling came over Holly as she stared at Mum from a distance. It was almost as though she was looking at a stranger, as if Mum wasn't really her Mum but someone that Holly didn't know at all.

Has she changed, Holly thought, suddenly grown older and I haven't noticed?

Or have I changed?

Then Mum spotted her and waved.

Holly raised her hand and gave a little wave back. She thought about the photo of Jay on her phone. Should I show her? she wondered.

No, she decided. Jay's mine. I'm keeping him to myself.

Chapter 11
Lunch

"There you are," Mum said. "Thought you'd never get here. What on earth have you been up to?"

"Nothing much," said Holly.

Mum was staring at her through lidded eyes, a wary look on her face. "Jacket then lunch, all right?" she said.

Holly nodded and gave a small grin, "OK."

Mum's face relaxed with relief and she smiled back. "Where to first? *Melody's Boutique* or *Polka Dots*?

Holly turned her mouth down. "They're so last year." I sound just like Madison, she thought with an inward grin. "Everyone goes to *WestEast Street* now."

Mum shrugged. "Never been in there but if that's what you want, let's do it."

"OK," said Holly and they walked off into the Mall.

WestEast Street was at the far end and usually when Holly went shopping with Mum they would stop and scan the window displays, comment on what they liked and what was weird or just boring. But to Holly's relief

Mum walked straight past all the shops today.

Let's get this over and then I can get back to Jay, she thought. She wasn't even excited about getting a new jacket. Who cares? was all she could think as she strode forward, slightly ahead of Mum, as if she couldn't be bothered to walk together.

"This is it," Holly said, turning into the doorway of a shop without glancing back.

"All right," grumbled Mum. "Wait for me."

Holly stopped, hands in her pockets, head tipped to one side. She could almost feel Mum getting annoyed behind her. It's a bit stupid going shopping with my Mum at my age, she couldn't help thinking.

"Hey Holly," a voice called out from further inside the shop.

Looking up Holly saw Becca Wilson, with a couple of other girls from school. Her heart sank.

"All right?" she said, glancing over her shoulder. Fortunately Mum was thumbing through a rack of jackets against the wall.

Becca came over, her sly eyes looking Holly up and down. "That's nice, shopping with your Mum," she said, with a smirk on her face.

The other girls tittered and Holly felt herself go brick red.

"Did you hear about Amy?" Becca went on.

"What about Amy?" snapped Holly but inside she felt a stab. Do Becca and Amy message each other? Why don't I know about that?

"Got a hot boyfriend. Gabe. Amy sends me pics all the time." Becca threw a smug look at the other girls who smirked back.

"I know about Gabe," said Holly, with a shrug. She turned on her heel and walked away, hoping that was the end of it.

But Becca hadn't finished. "She said you messaged that boy, Jay, the one I did the Shoutout for. I didn't bother. Didn't fancy him."

Holly felt herself stiffen but she didn't turn back or reply.

So Amy and Becca saw my first messages with Jay, she thought. Not surprising really but now we DM, keep it all private. No-one knows what we talk about. Jay would hate that. I've only told Ellen about us and she doesn't do much on social media and stuff. She'd rather be with her pets.

Then Holly had another thought. I bet Becca went after Jay and he saw straight through her, how horrible and sly and mean she is all the time.

That made her feel much better and she went over to join Mum.

"This one, this one, maybe this one," Mum was saying, holding out some jackets. "Not that one, not your colour."

Holly glared at her and grabbed the first jacket.

"Just saying," muttered Mum, her mouth set in a straight line.

Holly wrenched off her old jacket and pulled on the new one. It was dark blue and fitted well, with a hood and pockets on each side. It was warm enough without being too thick and heavy.

Mum was tweaking the bottom and standing back to admire her. "It's nice, but we never buy the first thing we see."

"It's fine," said Holly in an irritated voice. "Don't always have to do things the same way, do we?"

Mum looked taken aback and giving a sigh, said, "Don't you want to try on a couple of others?"

Becca's voice drifted back into the shop from the doorway and Holly couldn't stand another humiliating exchange. What if Madison and the Bezzies came past? Or even Ellen? Then she remembered Ellen had gone to visit Tim and she couldn't help wishing she was going to meet Jay this afternoon.

"Holly? Are you listening? What about this one?"

Mum was holding out a bright red jacket with daisies embroidered around the collar.

"You are joking!" spluttered Holly, suddenly enraged. "I'm not eleven."

What would Jay think if he saw me in *that*? she thought.

"All right. No need to speak to me like that," said Mum in a quiet voice.

Her face had a pinched look about it and for a moment Holly felt sorry she'd been rude yet again.

But then she told herself, Serves her right for not accepting I'm growing up. Jay understands, he *knows* me, he really does. Not like the olds who are just getting... well... older.

Holly shrugged and said, "I'll take this one if that's OK with you."

Her voice sounded sulky and for a moment she wondered why she was always miserable around Mum these days. But then she shrugged. It's the same for everyone, isn't it? Look at Jay's mum.

"Fine," said Mum and she walked off towards the till

without waiting for Holly.

By the time Holly had taken off the new jacket, put her old one back on and joined Mum at the till, Mum was tapping her phone. She didn't look up when Holly appeared.

Holly stood there feeling a mixture of anger and misery until Mum put her phone away and the assistant called them over. Without speaking, Mum paid for the jacket and walked out of the shop.

"Thanks," said Holly in a small voice. "I do like the jacket."

"Good. Deli on the Square?"

Holly nodded. It was their favourite café in the middle of the Mall. "I'm starving."

Mum perked up and said in her normal chatty voice, "No wonder you're such a misery. Did you have any breakfast? Your blood sugar must be rock bottom. Come on my girl. Lunch!"

Holly couldn't help grinning as Mum grabbed her arm and pulled her into the Deli.

Mum was chatting on, in full flow now, "So didn't you have a friend over this morning? Too busy to eat I suppose. Typical and now you're all droopy. Oh look. They've got those nice crusty rolls we like…"

Mum ran on and on and Holly smiled and nodded in the right places until they each had a tray of food and had found a table.

They sat down and unloaded filled rolls, drinks and cakes. Holly had chosen a strawberry milkshake – that's what Gabe and Amy like sharing, she thought. Maybe me and Jay could have a milkshake together one day.

She snapped the shake to send to Jay later.

"So was that the friend you had round this morning? That nice girl you bumped into in the shop just now?" Mum said, smiling at Holly as she took a bite out of her roll.

Holly spluttered down her straw. "Nice! That was Becca Wilson; about as mean as you can get."

"Oh." Mum had a puzzled look on her face.

Holly sighed. Mum couldn't help it. She sort of knew most things about Holly when Amy was here. Mum lost her best friend too when Amy and her family moved away. Their mums had been best friends the whole time they lived in the same street and they could both talk forever.

She put down her milkshake and said in a slow voice, "Look, I'm not friends with Becca but we're in the same year at school. Another girl from my year, Ellen, came round for an hour this morning. And just for the record, I'm not friends with Noah Levy either. But yes, I do look out for him in school since you asked me."

Mum's face relaxed. "Good, that's all good and just for the record, I know you're growing up, Holly and that's OK too." She gave Holly her brilliant smile, the one that Holly always felt she kept just for her and for a moment Holly felt warmed as if the sun was out here inside the Mall.

Then Mum's phone pinged. She grabbed it and swiped, muttering to herself, "Now what?"

Holly picked up her phone too and read through Jay's messages while she ate her roll. He kept saying how lonely he was without her and how long would she be with her Mum and then he wrote a string of messages about missing Mike.

Holly felt close to tears when Mum interrupted her thoughts.

"Gran's sent me a long shopping list. We have to go to the supermarket this afternoon."

No way, thought Holly. "Homework," she muttered.

"Oh, OK," said Mum.

They finished their lunch without talking much.

Holly's phone pinged almost continuously and Mum kept giving her funny looks but Holly kept her head down.

After lunch they caught the bus back home. Mum let them into the house and Holly ran straight upstairs and threw herself on her bed with a huge sigh of relief.

Free at last, she almost shouted out loud.

"Just going to the supermarket," Mum called out from below.

"OK," Holly called back.

She listened to the door opening and then closing again.

Finally!!

holly: RU there??

jay: yep

holly: mum gone out to the supermarket

jay: they take up a lot of UR time

   : UR mum and dad

holly: yep

jay: U need time to yourself

holly: dont think they get it

jay: B VERY CLEAR * sticker: boy saying BRUTAL*

   : gotta be cruel 2 be kind

holly: haha

jay: not saying they dont love U and stuff but do they really
    get U??
    : like I get U
holly: NOOO!!
jay: *thumb up emoji*
holly: they dont even know about U jay
jay: not their business
    : we R private!!
    : just U and me beautiful holly

Holly glowed. He keeps calling me beautiful, she thought and caught her reflection in the mirror. Her eyes seemed to sparkle and there was a smile on her face which made her cheeks shine in the light. Maybe I *am* attractive, she told herself, with a rush of happiness.

And Jay was so right about Mum and Dad. They take up far too much time, she thought. But she had to admit, apart from a boring lunch with Mum and bumping into Becca, it had been a wonderful day so far.

Thinking of Becca made her wonder if Jay and Becca still messaged. Can't hurt to ask, she told herself.

holly: so U and becca still friends?

There was no answer. Holly stared at her screen. Jay wasn't even typing. She shook her phone. Was something wrong with the connection? But no, there were three bars. Five minutes passed by. What have I done wrong? she asked herself over and over.

Then to her relief she saw Jay was typing.

jay: who said anything about becca?

holly: she did
    : when i was shopping with mum
jay: shes a nasty little liar * angry red face emoji*

Holly stared at the screen in shock.

jay: U there
holly: yep
    : RU angry with me?

She felt close to tears. I've messed it all up. I don't know how to *be* around a boy, do I? There was another long pause and then to her relief the screen lit up.

jay is typing...

jay: just dont like liars
    : surprised U listen to nasty girls like becca
    : she sent me a message but i didnt reply
    : cos of U holly

Of course, thought Holly. I should have known. Jay was still typing.

jay: but if U want to be with nasty becca or UR mum and
    dad
    : instead of me
    : nothing i can do
Holly: NOOOO!!!! i hate becca
    : she went on 2 me about U
    : didnt tell her anything
jay: did U show her my pic??

holly: god no! why would i?
     : mum and dad are old and boring and i dont have any
      real friends since amy left
     : theres only U Jay

She waited and waited. Fifteen minutes dragged by on her clock. It felt like fifteen hours. She began to plan the rest of her life without Jay; all alone as Gran's Crisis got worse and worse; sitting with Ellen and Tim at lunch while they talked about animals and going out together...

Her phone pinged and her heart gave a jolt.

jay: gotta go
holly: sorry jay so sorry

But no matter how much she stared at her screen there were no more messages from Jay.

Chapter 12
Amy

Holly had finished English and Science homework by the time Mum arrived back home. There was still nothing from Jay so she went downstairs and helped to unpack the car.

"Thanks darling," said Mum, as they brought in the last two bags. "I'll pop the kettle on and we'll have a nice cuppa."

There was the sound of the front door opening and Dad called out, "I'm home."

"In here," called back Mum.

She rummaged about in one of the bags and pulled out a cake in a box. "Ta dum! Family treat."

Holly couldn't help smiling and then Dad came in and dropping an arm around her shoulders, he pretended to lean on her, saying, "Prop up your old man after a hard day at the office."

"Da-ad," said Holly, with a laugh.

Dad took off his suit jacket and loosened his tie. They all sat down. Mum poured tea and handed out plates with huge slices of chocolate cake.

"Homework all done, Hol Pol?" asked Dad.

"In your dreams," groaned Holly.

For once she wished she could just heave it all back in her bag and concentrate on Jay. *If only I hadn't gone shopping with Mum, or at least hadn't said anything about Becca. Jay wouldn't have disappeared,* she kept telling herself.

There were still no messages. It had been over two hours.

"Better go back up," said Holly.

"Dinner at six," said Mum. "Steak and chips. Your Dad's doing the steak."

"Onions and mushrooms?" said Holly, as she went towards the hall.

"Course," called out Dad. "So don't be late!"

Holly ran upstairs and laid her phone on her desk where she could see the screen instantly. It was so hard to concentrate on homework when she was worrying about Jay but in the end she decided Maths would take her mind off everything.

She spent the next hour on homework and then they all had dinner together on their laps, sitting in front of the Saturday comedy show. By ten o'clock Holly's eyes were closing and Mum sent her up to bed.

Her last thought before she fell asleep was, *Where's my Jay?*

She was dreaming about meeting Amy in the Mall when a noise sounded in her ears. Waking up, she realised her phone was pinging. It was gone two o'clock; the middle of the night.

Jay! she thought and grabbed her phone.

jay: RU awake?

   : holly

   : wake up

   : im so lonely

   : missing U

holly: im here

    : RUOK??

jay: no

holly: whats up??

jay: phone ran out of juice and lost my charger

   : took hours to find it

Holly: oh ok

jay: U angry with me??

Holly: no course not

    : missed U 2

    : thought you were angry with me about becca

jay: shes not worth it

   : what did U do without me??

Holly: not much just homework

    : dinner and tv with mum and dad

jay: that must have been boring

Holly paused. It had been a nice evening with Mum and Dad and for once they had all chilled out and there were no rows. But if I tell Jay that he might think I'm a bit of baby, she thought.

holly: yep would rather be with U

jay: course you would

   : just wanna hang with U all the time now

holly: same

jay: dont want to stop U being with your family

Did she really mean it? Well, if it was a choice between Jay and Mum and Dad, Jay came out on top every time. The only reason she stayed downstairs after dinner was because Jay had gone so quiet. Now he'd explained what happened, she wanted to be with him as much as possible.

They messaged for over two hours until Holly fell asleep, her phone in her hand. She woke up as Mum came in, saying, "Time to get up, darling. We're going to Gran's, remember?"

Holly rolled over and opened her eyes. It was almost nine and her phone was completely dead. The thought of all day at Gran's where the signal was intermittent was already annoying her. She'd warned Jay in the night that she might not be able to message very much and he seemed to accept it. But she knew he didn't like to be cut off from her. Especially as it was less than a week to Mike's anniversary.

She swung her legs out of bed and put her phone on charge. After a quick shower, she pulled on jeans and a sweat shirt and grabbed her school bag. Maybe I can do a bit of homework after lunch, she thought. Gran's bound to want to watch TV with mum.

After breakfast Dad drove them to Gran's. As they left Brighton and rolled through the countryside to the village, Holly stared out of the window. It was a grey, drizzly day and Dad put on the heater to keep the windows from steaming up. Gazing at the clean bare fields rising in a gentle slope to the sky, Holly found herself wondering what Amy was doing. If Amy hadn't left, she'd be coming with us today.

She stared down at her phone. It had charged to 50% before they left.

In an impulse she messaged her friend.

Holly: hey whats new?

There was no answer. Holly checked her watch. It was ten thirty and then she remembered that Canada was five hours back. Amy was still asleep.

Holly sighed. Maybe Amy will message when she wakes up. It's Sunday morning over there too, so no school. Unless she had a sleepover last night which meant she'd be busy all morning.

Gran was so pleased to see them she chattered on non-stop. Just like Mum, Holly thought with a sigh.

Holly helped Dad to bring in the shopping and Mum unpacked in the tiny kitchen.

Holly had only been to the cottage a couple of times since Grandpa had died and now she could see how empty it must feel. No Grandpa and no Lucy sniffing round their feet and bounding outside. It made her feel so sorry for Gran, trying to 'go it alone'.

"I could come up on the bus and see you after school one day," Holly said, trying to think of something to cheer Gran up.

"That would be nice darling. Wait until we sort out all the heating problems. Your mum's coming up this week to meet the engineer." Gran looked tired and drawn as if it was all too much for her.

"OK," said Holly. "Any time. It's not far."

But secretly she was rather pleased. There was no signal in the cottage and she'd much rather be at home after school, messaging Jay.

She wondered if the signal was better in the garden.

Mum kept her busy for the next hour sorting out Gran's cupboards and then taking her chance when everyone went upstairs to check on the hot water tank, Holly slipped out into the long straggly back garden and walked to the fence which bordered the wood at the end.

The signal was a bit better and she messaged Jay.

holly: at grans but signal awful
   : RUOK
Jay: miserable without U
  : do U have to stay??

Holly stared at the screen, puzzled. Of course she had to stay. They'd come to support Gran. Mum had given her a big lecture in the car about keeping Gran cheerful today and not doing anything to upset her. Holly knew she meant not getting into a mood again.

holly: yep gran needs us
Jay: OK

The signal disappeared. Holly opened the back gate and went into the wood. She couldn't remember ever going there by herself. She was always with Grandpa, Gran and Lucy and often Amy too. She found the blackened ring of stones where they used to make fires and there was the path she and Amy would explore. The wood was very small so they never got lost. Once they were out of sight of the grown-ups they could pretend they were discovering a new planet or trekking through the rain forest.

Life was so much less complicated when I was a kid, thought Holly. I was never alone and I always had a best friend.

Her phone pinged but as she stared at the screen she saw it wasn't Jay.

amy: hey U howz it going???
holly: *smiley emoji* good
    : U?? and the hot gabe??
amy: * laughing emoji*
    : bit weird having a boyfriend
    : really missing U holly
holly: looks like U have lotta new mates
amy: sort of but

The signal faded and Holly waved her phone around in the air. So Amy hadn't forgotten about her and it didn't sound as if everything was as wonderful as it seemed from all the photos.

Her phone pinged again.

amy: tough making it in a new country
    : have to make a big effort with the other girls
    : they all have their groups
    : sooo lonely without U
    : dont have a best friend like U holly

Holly felt her mood soar as she read Amy's words. She's missing me as much as I'm missing her!

holly: what about gabe??
amy: cant have a boyfriend as a best friend!!

The signal faded and this time it didn't return. Holly walked back towards the house, wondering what Amy really meant. Doesn't she like Gabe the way I like Jay? she asked herself.

She couldn't imagine her life without Jay now. She told him everything, especially in the middle of the night when the house was quiet and it felt as though she and Jay were the only two people alive in the world.

She told him how she hated her skin and her teeth, how her Mum and Gran were way more attractive than she was, how she wished she was thinner and taller. Every time she had a row with Mum and Dad, he was the first person she told and he always comforted her and told her how wonderful she was.

She'd taken a screenshot of her favourite message and saved it. Now as she walked back across the lawn, she read through it again.

jay: UR beautiful holly
   : luv UR skin an UR teeth
   : luv UR hair an UR smile
   : i think UR PERFECT!!!
   : im always here for you
   : my beautiful holly

The message made her glow with happiness.

As she pushed open the kitchen door and stepped into the cottage, Dad called out, "The fresh air's doing you the world of good, Hol Pol. Look at those rosy cheeks!"

"Our Holly's always had beautiful cheeks," said Gran, in her rich, warm voice.

Holly gave her a big smile and caught Mum's eye. She was staring at Holly in that wary way again but then she gave a sigh and smiled back. "Lunch everyone. Sit down."

I'll walk down the street later, thought Holly. The signal will be better there and I can tell Jay that Amy's been in touch. He'll be so pleased, won't he?

Holly helped Mum wash up and then she muttered about going out for a walk.

"What about homework?" said Mum and her voice had a bit of an edge to it.

Holly frowned and growled back, "All right, keep your hair on."

She could feel Mum stiffen beside her and a puzzled look came over Gran's face.

"That's not like you, darling," her grandmother said.

Holly stood there for a moment and then suddenly it was as though she was suffocating in the small room. Dad was screwing back a loose cupboard door and Mum was trying to put plates away behind him. She couldn't stand it any longer.

"Sor–*ree*," she said, tossing her hair back over her shoulder and before anyone could snap at her, she went out of the house and down the path.

Can't they get off my back? she fumed as she pulled her phone out of her pocket. The signal was strong and her phone pinged twice.

jay: where RU?

holly: still at gran * frowning emoji *

jay: cant U get a bus home

holly: theyd go mad at me

jay: so what? i need U

holly: so does gran

jay: shes got UR mum and dad

    : im very lonely

holly: so sorry jay

jay: need U so much babes

holly: always here for U

jay: xxx

The kisses made Holly feel warm all over. He really cares about me. Must tell him about Amy, she reminded herself. He'll be so pleased, won't he?

holly: guess what

jay: hate guessing

holly: oh sorry

    : amy messaged and said shes missing me

    : isnt that great??!!??

There was a pause and Holly checked the signal. It was still strong. She waited. Several minutes passed before her screen lit up again.

jay is typing ...

jay: i dont think its great

    : she must have a slow time

    : no one else around

Holly stared at the screen, confused. What does he mean? Amy doesn't really care about me? A little worm of doubt began to wriggle through her mind.

jay: RU there?

holly: yep

    : don't understand

    : amy was happy to chat

jay: yeah sure she is

  : when it suits her

  : all im saying is why now??

  : she left U all alone for so long

holly: see what U mean

jay: just looking out for U babes

  : dont want U to get hurt again

  : im always here and will NEVER let U down

holly: im here for U2 jay FOREVER!!!

Chapter 13
Confession
on the Sea Wall

OMG!! No, no, nooo!!

Heavy with sleep, Holly stared in horror at the numbers on her digital clock.

08:36

She'd overslept by a whole hour!

Throwing back the covers, she leapt out of bed, splashed her face in the bathroom and pulled on her uniform in record time.

"Mu- um! Why didn't you wake me?" Holly called out as she ran downstairs.

But there was only silence. The house was empty. Mum and Dad must have gone out early and left her alone.

So what else is new? she thought, as she grabbed her coat and bag and ran out of the house.

There was already a bus at her stop and she just managed to leap on before the doors closed. But as she dropped onto a seat and scrabbled about in her bag, she realised she'd forgotten her charger. Her phone was completely dead. She and Jay had messaged last night for hours.

We're going to have another whole day out of touch. The thought sent a wave of misery through her. Should I go back home? she wondered. But she was already very late.

For a fleeting moment she considered skipping school but shook the thought out of her head. She and Amy never did anything like that.

As the bus swayed and jerked through the traffic, Holly began to imagine how angry Jay would be tonight. But he'd probably be even more angry if I skipped off, she told herself. Jay's like me. He'd never do that.

The bus arrived and Holly leapt off, running down the road as fast as she could. The street was empty. Even the stragglers had made it into the playground before her. Then her heart sank. Miss Holland, the PE teacher, was on gate duty.

Holly arrived panting and pushed her hair out of her eyes. "Sorry Miss," she said in a breathless voice.

The PE teacher glared at her. "How many times late this term?" Then she wrote something on the clipboard in her hand.

"Never been late before."

The teacher narrowed her eyes at Holly. "So, never had a phone confiscated, never been late and then suddenly I catch you doing both in a few days. Is there something you need to tell me?"

Holly shook her head. "It won't happen again."

She stared back at Miss Holland and then slowly she

pushed her lower lip out like – well – Becca Wilson or her mates; the ones who backchat the teachers and never care if they get into trouble.

But I don't care today, she told herself. All I care about is not being able to message Jay.

Miss Holland scribbled on a slip of paper and handed it to her. "Detention, Tuesday night. Inform your parents."

Holly took the slip and started to walk past into the playground.

The teacher blocked her way with her broad, muscular form. "I'm watching you, Holly Bennett."

Holly stared at the ground and waited for the teacher to move. Then she walked off, slinging her bag higher along her arm, shoulders back, as if to say, Am I bothered?

She almost wished Becca Wilson was there to see her standing up to a teacher.

It was a horrible morning. Holly couldn't concentrate on anything; she'd forgotten her Maths homework – after all that work, she moaned to herself – and was threatened with yet another detention. The boys she sat with in Science smirked at her across the room.

Looking away she caught Madison's eye. Aisha was sitting next to Madison and she leaned over and whispered something in the other girl's ear, nodding towards Holly. Madison pursed her lips and looked down.

Her face burning, Holly wished she could disappear through the floor. It was a relief when lunchtime came.

"No chips today," called out Ellen in an almost cheery voice, as Holly arrived at their table and dumped her tray.

Ellen was waving a tuna sandwich in the air. There was a yoghurt and banana on her plate too.

Holly sat down with an approving smile. "Very healthy."

"Dad's given me money for new uniform. I'm off to the Mall after school. Come with me Holly, please."

Holly hesitated. She needed to get back and charge her phone.

But Ellen was staring at her with those big blue eyes and the buttons on her shirt were barely meeting in the middle today.

Relenting Holly said, "Course. But only for a bit. Need to get home."

"Excellent," said Ellen.

As they ate Ellen filled Holly in about her visit to Tim on Saturday. "...and he even mentioned how nice I looked." She lowered her eyes and pushed a sandwich around her plate.

"Awesome," said Holly.

Ellen shot her a grin and then released a torrent of words about the visit; how lovely Tim's family were and such lurid descriptions of the goats that Holly felt sick.

As Ellen paused for breath, Holly said, "So are they farmers?"

"No, it's like a smallholding. They keep bees and sell honey but they have quite a big house with six bedrooms..."

"Six! They must be minted."

"No, I don't think so," said Ellen. "His mum and dad are sort of hippies, you know, alternative. They don't eat meat and his dad has a pony tail."

"Oh, right," said Holly and they grinned at each other.

"The house is a bit tumble down, crumbling at the

edges and the kitchen's really old fashioned with like tons and tons of crockery and none of it matches. They do bed and breakfast 'to make ends meet' Tim says."

Ellen flipped open her yoghurt.

Holly heard a commotion behind her and craning round she saw Rick elbow into Noah's side. Noah nearly dropped his tray and a wave of laughter swept round the room.

Not again, she thought with an impatient sigh but Noah was left standing in the middle of the room all alone, staring at the floor. Ellen was picking cucumber out of her sandwich and there was nowhere else Holly could see with spaces.

"Hey, Noah, over here," she called out.

Noah shot her a grateful look and coming over, he sat down next to her, fumbling with his things.

Holly glanced at Ellen but she was moving to make room for Tim who had appeared, pulling his earphones out.

"All right?" said Tim, nodding to Noah and Holly.

Noah kept his head down but Holly nodded back and suddenly she was sitting in a group and everyone seemed – well – OK about it.

Tim and Ellen were swiping their phones and showing each other photos, when Noah dropped his knife and it clattered onto his plate.

"Sorry," he muttered.

Tim looked over and said, "You're in the Advanced Maths class, aren't you?"

Noah nodded.

"What's that?" asked Ellen.

Noah didn't speak so Tim said, "That's the class for kids who're really clever, like –gifted, isn't it, Noah?"

Noah still didn't look up but he nodded.

There was a pause and then Holly said, "That's cool. I really struggle with algebra."

Noah raised his head and said, "I could help you."

She noticed for the first time that he had really lovely eyes, warm and dark like his mother's. He never pushes himself forward, she thought, but he's actually super intelligent.

Tim was looking at Noah with respect. "I tried out for it," said Tim. "But the test was unbelievable. You must be really good to get through."

"I suppose so," said Noah in a quiet voice.

Ellen gave a short laugh and she and Tim started looking at photos again.

While they were busy, Noah turned to Holly and said, with lowered eyes, "Something's happened."

"Oh," said Holly.

"With Rick."

"What?"

Noah was about to answer when a huge commotion broke out in the middle of the hall. People start to shout, "Fight! Fight!" Two younger boys were pushing each other against the tables and plates crashed to the floor. Holly watched as the teachers waded in and separated the boys, marching them out of the dining hall.

Then the bell went for afternoon school and Holly stood up.

"Talk about it later?" she said to Noah who hadn't moved.

He gave a small nod.

Afternoon school seemed to pass more quickly and

then Holly was walking to the bus stop with Ellen. On the bus to the Mall she spotted Noah huddled in a corner, swiping his phone. His face looked pinched and miserable but Holly couldn't catch his eye.

What's happened? she wondered. Is Rick sending him horrible messages? I'll ask him when we get off the bus. But she could almost hear Jay's voice in her ear saying, Don't get involved.

"Good friend of yours?" Ellen asked.

Holly swivelled round. Did she mean Jay? But Ellen was staring towards Noah. She shrugged not sure if Noah was an actual friend. After all, it was Mum who'd asked her to look out for him.

If I don't want to get involved, why do I feel so guilty? she couldn't help wondering. She could almost hear Amy's voice in her ear, *Bullying is everyone's responsibility.*

Amy was always there for me, she told herself. But now I'm all alone.

Except for Jay.

And Ellen and Tim?

So why not Noah too?

The bus arrived at the Mall while Holly was in the middle of all these thoughts and she followed Ellen out onto the street. She felt a shove from behind and turning she saw Noah pushing past, swinging his school bag at anyone who didn't move quickly enough, a look of complete fury on his face. His ears were lit up like traffic lights as he zigzagged across the road, dodging cars and ran down towards the beach.

This doesn't look good, she told herself with an inward sigh. If he's going to meet Rick in that mood there might be a fight and Noah definitely won't win.

She grabbed Ellen's arm. "Go and get started, I'll just be a couple of minutes."

Before Ellen could say anything, Holly took off at a jog after Noah. As she reached the crossing on the Promenade road, the sea stretching grey and flat ahead of her, Noah was on the other side. He was running fast now and she was already puffing. She didn't have the breath to call out to him and anyway, he was too far ahead to hear.

Noah ran to the steps opposite the Queens Hotel and then down to the old stone walkway which ran over ninety metres across the beach and out into the sea.

The walkway had a huge round stone sculpture near the end with a hole in the middle. Everyone called it the Donut. When the sea was rough it would spray straight through the hole. She and Amy used to love standing there as little kids, hoods up, screaming at every wave, the taste of salt on their lips and sea spray soaking their faces.

Why's he going down there? she thought. She scanned the walkway but it was empty. No sign of Rick Gold or anyone else.

Then to her horror she saw Noah throw his bag down – it landed in a puddle but he didn't seem to care – and climb up on the stone wall. He tried standing on it but it was too narrow, so he sat down, both legs dangling over the sea.

Is he crazy? she thought in a panic. It must be a five metre drop to the beach. He'll break his neck or at least his legs!

Without waiting for the lights to go red, Holly

charged across the road and down the steps to the walkway, yelling, "Noah! Get down! Don't be stupid!"

Noah didn't even turn but his whole body leaned towards the drop beneath him.

One false move, thought Holly, her heart pounding in her chest.

It had begun to rain, long sheets of water washing over the ground and turning the sea wall slippery. Holly had her new jacket on so at least the hood wasn't leaking but her skirt was already drenched.

I've got to get him down, she thought, as she began to shiver.

Noah didn't seem to notice the rain. His hood was down and his hair was already soaked.

As Holly came up she could see his face was wet as though tears were spurting out again. Only Noah wasn't crying. His head was turned to one side and she could see a numb, robotic look on his face.

She called up, "Is it Rick? Honestly Noah, he's not worth it."

Noah swivelled his head and stared down into Holly's eyes. Holly stared back trying not to blink which was difficult through the rain.

Maybe I can *will* him to get down, she thought.

Then Noah shouted, "You don't steal, you don't cheat anybody, you don't…"

"…what?" cut in Holly. "What're you going on about?"

"You heard!" Noah shouted back. "*Everyone* heard me!"

Holly looked around. "There's no-one here, you muppet."

"Everyone that mattered heard me!" he yelled back

over the roar of the waves. "Everyone heard me say it. They heard every single word..."

His voice broke down.

He sounds like one of those nutters who stand on street corners telling you to repent, Holly thought. Only she wasn't sure if Jews did that sort of thing.

Then Noah took a deep breath and roared, "Don't defraud ANYBODY. Don't commit robbery."

He stopped and shifted his legs, swaying on the wall. For a second she was certain he would fall.

Holly took a step forward but Noah steadied himself.

Then he said, "I did all that and now I'm a common thief."

"What did you do?" asked Holly.

"Shoplifting," said Noah and then it was as though all the air went out of his body. He dropped his head, swayed slightly and his shoulders slumped.

Holly grabbed him and with all her strength, lifted him down onto the pavement. Her body shook with the effort and she leaned against the wall. Noah stood very still, hands in his pockets, his face white as plaster and pinched with cold.

"That was dead stupid!" cried out Holly.

"Doesn't matter, nothing does," said Noah in a numb voice.

Holly stared at him for a moment and then she grabbed his arm and said, "Come on."

He didn't move so she hoisted his bag onto her shoulder – it weighed a ton – and tugging hard, pulled him along the street to a café. Pushing open the door she dragged Noah inside and onto a chair in the window.

"Stay there," she commanded.

Then she went and bought two coffees and a chocolate bar. As she waited for the coffees she glanced at her watch. Quarter past four. Jay would be messaging and messaging. She needed to get home and what about Ellen?

But as she went back to the table and sat down, Noah's chalk white face pushed all these thoughts away.

"Drink!" she said, wrapping her frozen hands around her cup.

Noah sipped at the coffee and after a while some colour began to creep back into his cheeks. He picked up the chocolate and then dropped it back on the table.

"Was it with Rick?" Holly said. "The shoplifting?"

Noah nodded.

"What did you take?"

"Chocolate bar, giant one. Rick distracted the shopkeeper."

"OK," said Holly.

She looked down at her cup, feeling quite shocked. Nice little Noah actually stealing? Who would've thought it?

When she looked up again, Noah had his big dark eyes fixed on her.

"Can't be worth much. One chocolate bar," she said.

"You don't understand," Noah burst out. "How can I look anyone in the eye again? Mum and Dad, my brothers, Daniel."

"Who?"

"Our rabbi."

"Oh."

She couldn't remember anyone calling a vicar by his first name. Not that her family went to church or anything. Amy's family were Catholic and always called the priests Father something or other.

"Don't you call him rabbi or sir?" she couldn't help asking.

Noah almost smiled, which was a relief. "No, we just call him Daniel."

He looked Holly straight in the eye, "My barmitzvah portion was Leviticus 19. It's about not stealing. But I'm a criminal now and the shopkeeper's poorer because of me. How can I make a speech at Ben's barmitzvah on Saturday? I'm not morally justified."

"That's a bit strong," said Holly.

"There's no excuse for stealing unless you're starving and being persecuted. That's what I said in synagogue last year before I read out my portion. I said it in front of the whole community. I can *never* face them again."

He turned his head to look out of the window and Holly cast about in her mind for something to say.

"OK," she said, "but look, you obviously regret it and that's a good thing, isn't it?"

Noah shrugged, his face a chunk of misery.

"So make sure you don't do it again," said Holly.

"Rick's pushing me to shoplift today. He was messaging me on the bus. He wants me to steal a load of USB sticks from a shop in the Mall. They have security guards there. I'll get caught and then I've had it. Rick and his crew sell all their stolen stuff in school."

"Just say no," said Holly with a frown.

Noah shook his head. "He said he'd tell Daniel if I refused."

"Well so what?" said Holly. "You didn't rob a bank. I mean, it's only a bar of chocolate."

"Would you shoplift?"

"No, but that's not the point."

"It is!" cried out Noah. "No-one I know would shoplift or steal anything."

"Except Rick."

Noah nodded. "He's got in with this crew in Y11, they're really bad. He's been getting into trouble since his parents' divorce last year. I heard Mum and Dad talking about it. I don't know what to do Holly, I really don't."

They sat in silence for a minute and then Holly had a thought.

"Go and tell Daniel yourself."

Noah frowned and stared down into his cup. When he looked back his eyes suddenly seemed much brighter. "That's amazing. You're so right. I'll speak to him before Rick does."

He pulled his phone out of his pocket and tapped furiously. "I've sent Daniel an email saying I have to see him urgently."

You can email rabbis? thought Holly. Weird.

They finished their drinks and as they stood up to leave Noah's phoned pinged. "It's Daniel. I can see him now. He's in the synagogue. Only…"

"What?"

"Rick told me to meet at the Mall."

"You're not going," said Holly. "Stuff Rick, I'll walk you to the bus stop, right?"

She bunched her fist and held it out. Noah hesitated for a moment and then he bumped fists.

"You're a true friend, Holly," he said, a relieved grin on his face.

As they walked off, Holly thought, Noah's much more than a weepy boring boy. He's actually very honest and decent and we're friends.

A warm glow spread through her.

Then she remembered Jay and breaking into a run, sprinted back to her bus stop, pulling her pass out. I'll have to send Ellen a message when I get home, she thought. No time to find her in the Mall.

Jay will understand when I tell him what happened with the charger and then with Noah.

But there was a tight knot in her stomach.

Chapter 14
Stranger at the Door

jay: U wanna be with your friends
   : not me
holly: nooo!!! its not like that

They'd been messaging for over an hour. Holly had her phone on charge and was sitting in the kitchen devouring a multi-pack of crisps, feeling steeped in misery. Jay was so mad at her and she didn't know what to say.

As usual Mum was out and there was no dinner. The knot in her stomach seemed to tighten as she swallowed, tapping and tapping her apologies to Jay. Her phone felt as though it was on fire in her hand. Can phones explode from overuse? she couldn't help wondering.

jay is typing...

jay: U cant have it both ways
holly: dont understand

jay: its ok if U wanna be with your friends

: not me

: but i thought we were special

holly: we R

: not my friends just kids from school

jay: thought U said they were all idiots

holly: they R

: would much rather be with U

jay: doesnt feel like it

: feels the opposite

: feels like they just click and U run

holly: no never

: ellen needed me 2 go shopping

: noah was upset

jay: IM UPSET!!

: MY MATE DIED

: im all alone

: an U gone all cold on me babes

Holly stopped typing, her eyes blurred with tears. Jay had said so often in the past few days that none of her friends cared about her. She was beginning to think he was right.

When Amy went to Canada and I was left all alone in school, looking miserable, I don't remember any of them coming over to me, she told herself. Not Ellen or Tim or Noah.

Jay kept on complaining about her so-called friends, she kept agreeing and apologising and begging him to believe her. But he wouldn't make up.

We're over, she told herself, during a long silence. I'm dumped.

Her phone pinged.

jay: *sticker: boy on a sofa saying CUDDLES?*

Holly stared at the screen and her face split into a grin.

jay: * sticker: boy grinning and saying CRAZY ABOUT YOU!*

Holly's heart did a little jump. She grabbed her phone and started typing.

Holly: me 2
      : im crazy about U jay
      : i know UR right about the other kids
      : they dont get me
      : they R not real friends like U
jay: told U babes
    : gotta listen 2 me
    : jay knows best
holly: amy sent another pic of gabe today
      : i didnt answer
      : sick of her and gabe!!
jay: YAAY!!!
    : i luv ya so much xxx
holly: luv U2 xxxx

The doorbell rang, sounding through the empty, silent house.

Holly looked up.

It was past seven and very dark outside. The rain had become heavier and the gutters in the street would be flowing like small rivers by now. The trees outside the kitchen window were bending in the strong wind as rain lashed against the glass. Another storm was blowing up from the sea. Why would anyone go out on a night like this?

She felt as if every cell in her body was listening. The doorbell sounded again, more impatient this time.

Jay was sending messages.

holly is typing...

holly: someone ringing the doorbell
    : only me home
jay: dont answer
holly: but what if its the neighbour
    : mum has an amazon parcel for them
jay: not safe
holly: can look thru the glass panel
    : see if its a stranger
jay: no holly

The doorbell rang again and then someone rapped on the door. It sounded quite a polite rap, like the sort of rap the people next door would do.

It's OK, Holly told herself and leaving her phone on the counter, she walked out into the hallway and towards the door. She could see a tall shape through the glass but she couldn't tell if it was a man or a woman.

As she reached the front door a voice called, "Anyone home?"

It sounded like the neighbour.

Reaching over, she released the door lock and peered round the crack in the doorway.

A man was standing on the step. He wore a black

leather jacket, shiny with rain and black jeans. She didn't recognise him.

"Is your mum home, love?" asked the man in a polite voice. His eyes were heavy lidded in a pale round face. "Need to discuss her home insurance." He held up a briefcase, also running with rain water.

Careful, she told herself. Don't say you're home alone. "We're not expecting you," she said.

The man frowned and checked his phone. "Hmm, appointment says today at this time."

He moved slightly as if to step into the house and in an instant Holly slammed the door and rammed the chain on.

"Ring her later!" she called through the door but her voice squeaked with terror.

Who is he? Why is he here? If Mum had an appointment tonight, she told herself, surely she would be home and not leave me to answer the door all alone.

But a part of her wasn't sure what Mum and Dad would do anymore. They were always out and the house creaked and creaked as the storm raged like a wild animal outside the door.

Holly walked back to the kitchen on wobbly legs and messaged Jay.

> holly: strange man at the door
>   : i slammed it shut
>   : my legs are shaking so much
>   : *frightened emoji*
> jay: thats dead scary
>   : so worried about U
>   : wanna come over and HUG U!!
> holly: aw thanks

: so glad got U 2 talk 2
: really really scared now
: massive storm and whole house creaking

jay: same here
: rain coming in under the front door

Does that mean Jay lives near the sea too? wondered Holly. I could ask him.

But then she paused. It was Monday night. She'd already decided that if they were still together on Wednesday – one week since they met – then she would tell Jay she lived in Brighton.

I'll wait till then, she decided, feeling sensible and responsible like they kept saying in school whenever they talked about the Internet.

jay is typing ...

jay: U there??
holly: yep
jay: so sorry babes
holly: fingers shaking when i type
jay: course
: wanna cheer U up
: HEY!! how about we have a pizza night???

Holly laughed out loud. That's what I love about Jay, she told herself. He can always cheer me up no matter how bad things are.

Love – she turned the word around in her mind. Am I in love? We sort of said we loved each other before but it didn't feel serious.

But now?

She wandered over to the freezer and opening the door, stared at the contents.

Am I in love? she wondered.

Madison said that she and Harry were in love this morning.

"Proper love," she told everyone. "We've exchanged rings."

She pulled out a chain hidden under her uniform and Holly could see a silver ring hanging, with a cluster of blue and red crystals.

"That is *so* gorgeous, Madison," said one of the Bezzies, with an envious sigh.

Holly had stared and stared at the ring. Imagine if Jay gave me a ring like that, she couldn't help thinking and a huge longing spread through her.

Madison was holding up her phone. There was a picture of a hand – a boy's hand – with a silver ring on the fourth finger. There was some lettering on the ring.

"That's Harry. It says, Love U Forever on it." Madison gave a happy sigh.

As they all moved off to class, Holly wondered if she should start looking for a ring for Jay. The thought sent excited flutters through her.

Now she unwrapped a pizza and put it in the oven. Then she poured herself a large glass of cola, snapped it and sent the pic to Jay.

holly: pizza in... having cola with you
jay: cheers babes!

Holly giggled and sipped her cola. It felt just as though Jay was in the room beside her. She fell into a daydream of bringing Jay home and Mum and Dad were out. We could do whatever we liked, she told herself. Without any interruption.

Then the doorbell sounded again.

Holly nearly dropped her glass. Her hands began to shake.

Who's that?

A massive gust blew round the house, rattling the windows and Holly half expected someone to burst through the back door. She grabbed her phone and pressed it to her chest as though in some way Jay could protect her.

The bell rang and rang. It was clear they weren't going to stop until someone opened the door. She crept out into the hall still clutching her phone. There was a blue light flashing through the glass panel in the front door.

Is it the police? she wondered.

Her phone pinged.

jay: hows UR pizza doing??
holly: door bell ringing again
  : i think the police R at the door
jay: what ?? why??
holly: dunno
  : weird
jay: super weird
holly: dont know what 2 do
  : should i open the door??
jay: yep

: but holly

: dont tell them about U and me

: its our secret

: cos what we have is so special we dont tell ANYONE

holly: course not

: too special to tell anyone

jay: good

: very good holly

: remember im right here

Holly stared at the screen as she walked towards the door, the bell ringing and Jay's messages of support streaming in.

A voice called out, "Police. Open up."

What if it's a hoax? she thought. "How do I know you're police?"

"Can't you see the police car?" growled the man behind the door.

Holly opened the door a crack, the chain still on. She called out, "Have you got, er, ID?"

The man muttered something under his breath and then shoved a card into her outstretched hand. Holly stared at a photo and the dark blue logo. Detective Inspector Rawlings the name read under the photo.

A hoarse voice called from the street. The man turned and shouted something back towards the police car.

They must be real police, Holly told herself and pushing the door shut, she released the chain and opened the door wide.

The man on the step was huge, six foot at least, wearing a hoody and jeans. His head was shaved and he carried a radio transmitter in his hand.

"Has anyone come to the door saying they had an appointment about insurance?" asked the man in an abrupt voice.

"Yes," said Holly. "About ten minutes ago."

The man nodded and spoke into his radio. "Got another one, Bob."

The phone crackled and the man went on, "Wearing a leather jacket and jeans?"

"Yes," said Holly.

"It's a scam," said the man. "Did you see which way they went?"

"No."

"OK." The man turned on his heel and sprinted down the path to the gate. He jumped into the police car and they took off down the road.

Holly watched them go. The time on her phone showed ten minutes past nine. Was anyone else going to ring the doorbell this evening?

She shivered at the thought and closing the front door went back into the kitchen.

Mum came home just after ten but by that time Holly was in bed, messaging Jay. Warm and safe under her duvet, Jay kept saying her Mum and Dad were no use anymore and Holly couldn't help agreeing. All sorts of people had thundered on the door, there'd been a horrible storm and the house creaked as if someone might break in. But no-one was home to keep her safe.

Only Jay was there to talk to, she told herself as she drifted off to sleep.

Chapter 15
Silence

"Ta dum!"

Ellen was waving her hands down her body as Holly sat down at their lunch table the next day.

"New uniform. What do you think?" said Ellen. "And what happened to you yesterday? I waited for ages at the Mall and then went shopping by myself."

Holly grinned and put her head on one side with an approving look, the one that Sandi used when she was picking a new top. "Very nice. Cool cardigan – like the buttons. Let's see the skirt."

Ellen stood up and did a twirl. A couple of older boys on the next table whooped and she blushed and sat down.

"See. You're getting all the attention now," said Holly.

"You like it?" said Ellen in a low voice.

Holly stared at the girl who had always seemed so mean and sulky. It's a transformation, just the kind that Sandi likes, she told herself and all because of me.

A swell of pride went through her.

"It's perfect," she said. "Sorry about yesterday. Family

crisis and my phone had gone dead. Oh look, here comes Tim."

Ellen looked round with an expectant smile as Tim appeared, pulling his earphones out. He stood for a second looking down at her.

Then he gave his little cough and said, "Um... new uniform?"

Ellen nodded, staring up at Tim with her wide blue eyes as if waiting for him to laugh or make a joke.

But Tim sat down and muttered, "Nice." He pulled at the sleeves of his blazer which ended above his wrists. "Could do with a new blazer, I suppose. Only ever had one."

"Since you started, like three years ago?" said Holly, almost choking on her sandwich. She had new uniform every year and one or two new bits every term.

"Dad doesn't believe in uniform," muttered Tim. "He's a pacifist. Says uniform's too military for his liking." Tim spoke in a soft Sussex burr which was even more pronounced than usual today.

As Holly unwrapped her sandwich, Noah slipped into the empty seat next to her.

Are we a lunch group now? she wondered. It gave her a warm, solid feeling inside. Much better than being alone and if she ate quickly there was still time to message Jay.

Ellen and Tim were deep in a discussion about caring for bees.

Holly said in a quiet voice to Noah, "All OK?"

Noah nodded. "Daniel was great. He took me straight to the shopkeeper and I confessed. I paid for the chocolate and he said he'd never had a kid do that before."

"That's all good then."

Noah nodded again. "I told Mum and Dad too and my brothers. It was OK."

"And Rick?"

"Stuff Rick." Noah clenched his lips together, his jaw set in a straight line.

Is he going to cry? wondered Holly. But his eyes were dry. There was a new, determined look on Noah's face and she couldn't help thinking again what lovely eyes he had.

Will Jay's eyes be that warm when we meet? she couldn't help thinking. Of course they will, she told herself. He's so lovely and caring, it'll be right there in his eyes.

"You could all come if you like." Tim's voice broke into her thoughts.

"Where?" said Holly.

"My place, see the puppies. We could go after school, only twenty minutes on the bus."

"Great," said Noah. "I'll come, how about you?"

Noah turned his dark eyes on Holly and she felt a flutter inside her. It's nice to have friends, she told herself. But I need to be with Jay.

"Can't, sorry," she said and was pleased to see Noah's look of disappointment.

It was Miss Holland's detention tonight. Holly had complained to Jay about it of course and he'd said she should skip it. It wasn't fair, she'd tried to get to school on time and he'd agreed.

Looking at Noah, she couldn't help thinking he was quite sweet when he wasn't crying. The thought made her feel mature now that she had a boyfriend.

"Oh come on Holly," said Ellen in her old impatient voice. "We won't let any teeth or claws near you."

"Sorry," said Holly, not wanting to admit she was in trouble. It all felt so childish. Maybe I'm growing out of school, she thought. It would be nice to be in college and not have to wear uniform anymore.

The others sighed and rolled their eyes.

Standing up with her phone in her hand, Holly said, "Laters."

But as she walked off her phone was strangely silent. No messages from Jay and when she sent a message there was no reply. She checked the signal, turned her phone off and on twice, sent message after message but there was still nothing.

The afternoon was busy with a Maths test. By the end of school she'd decided to skip the detention and concentrate on Jay. She could forge a note from Mum for Miss Holland about a dental appointment for toothache. She felt quite clever as she walked out of the gate, checking her phone. But there was still nothing from Jay.

What's happened? she wondered. Maybe he's had an accident, or something's happened to his Mum.

Or maybe he's angry with me. But why?

"Holly!" It was Ellen, with Tim and Noah. They were standing at the bus stop.

Holly went over, waving her phone. "Waiting for a message."

"Why don't you come with us," said Noah. "You can still message your friend."

Holly couldn't help noticing that Tim had one hand on his bike and the other slipped into Ellen's. Both of them were standing there as if this was nothing, quite normal, how they stood around all the time.

How would it feel to hold Jay's hand? wondered Holly. Where is he?

"Just come for an hour," said Ellen. "Still time to go home and do whatever you gotta do."

Holly hesitated and Tim said, "Bus is coming. Bet I beat you all home."

Noah and Ellen shouted after him as set off at speed, pumping his pedals.

The bus came to a halt and Holly made up her mind. "OK, just for a bit."

Noah's face broke into a smile and he stood back to let her on before him.

A perfect gentleman, she thought, as she stepped on the bus and swiped her pass.

Tim's home was outside the small village of Saddlescombe in the South Downs; wide chalk hills which lay north of Brighton and the sea. Gran's village was a mile or two away to the west. Tim had beaten them as he predicted and practically lifted Ellen down when they all arrived.

Flushed and laughing, Ellen shrieked, "Don't drop me, you nutter!"

Noah rolled his eyes at Holly.

"This way," said Tim.

Holly could see a path with no front gate or fence, leading up to a large square stone house standing on its own plot of land. There were wire fences on each side. The path was a mixture of chalk, flint and pebbles. Weeds pushed up through the ground and there were one or two quite big potholes.

They passed a battered jeep and other bits of machinery lying on the grass. Holly could see horses in a field in the distance but Tim said that was the neighbour's riding school.

"We have more land behind the house," he explained.

"That's where the bees and goats and chickens are kept," said Ellen.

"Nice," said Noah.

"Holly doesn't think so," said Ellen in a teasing voice.

Holly felt herself go red and Noah rolled his eyes at her again.

That made her feel better. I can't help it if I hate animals, she thought, just like Jay.

She checked her phone for the umpteenth time. Still no messages and now she could see there was a poor signal up here.

I'll just stay for a bit, she told herself. Then I'll take the bus back to civilisation.

Tim propped his bike up against the house and opening the front door – no key, Holly noticed, don't they keep it locked? – he led the way down a passage into the kitchen, a large room at the end of the house.

"Welcome to the madhouse," called out a man, taller than Holly's dad and thin like Tim, with long dark hair tied back in a ponytail. He wore mud-stained jeans and a blue sweater, with a large hole over the shoulder. The man was younger than Dad and way more cool, Holly couldn't help thinking. His face had that reddish, weathered look like Tim's – and like Grandad's used to be, she thought.

"Dad, meet Holly and Noah, you already know Ellen," said Tim.

At least his voice is properly broken, thought Holly, not ending in a squeak like Noah's.

"Nice to meet yer, now," said Tim's dad with a friendly grin. "Call me Pete."

Holly noticed he had a broader accent than Tim, drawing out his words in the old-fashioned Sussex way.

Like Grandad used to speak, she remembered with a sad pang. She missed Grandad's voice and his funny old Sussex words, like 'borstal' which meant a steep path up the Downs and even more weird, 'breadandcheese'.

"Old Billy now," Grandad would say, "breadandcheese friend so he is. Not like a good many; after what they can get."

"You gonna show your mates the pups?" asked Pete, breaking into Holly's thoughts.

"Yeah," said Tim and he and Ellen went out of the back door, Noah following.

Pete gave Holly an encouraging nod but she said, "Do you have Wi-Fi?"

"Sorry, love. It's down at the moment."

Holly's heart sank. How much longer could she dare to stay? Jay had been out of touch for hours.

She nodded to Pete and followed the others out of the door.

A large piece of land rising to a gentle slope opened up in front of her. There was an enclosure for the goats who were tugging at the ground and a couple of small outhouses where Holly could see hens roosting. Further away to the side were three white beehives.

I'm keeping well clear of those, she told herself with a shudder.

Beyond the end fence, all the way along the horizon were the South Downs, steep hills, wooded in places.

Flashes of white showed on the slopes where the chalk was laid bare.

It was a landscape Holly had known all her life from her grandparents' home and she loved the rolling hills as much as the rolling seas at Brighton.

Maybe Jay lives in Sussex and he sees all this too, she thought. I'm sure he loves it. We have so much in common, don't we?

"Over here, Holly," Tim called out.

Holly saw that the others were sitting on a heap of straw and old cushions with the stuffing coming out. In their arms were bundles of fur, mewling and snuffling. The puppies, Holly thought, her skin beginning to crawl.

"Sit down," commanded Ellen and before Holly knew it, she'd dropped a puppy into her lap.

Holly squealed and Ellen said, "Keep still or you'll make him nervous. Here." Ellen took Holly's hand. "Just stroke him gently and he'll go to sleep."

"Don't give me another one!" said Holly. Noah and Tim had at least three each in their laps.

Two much larger dogs, one an Alsatian which terrified Holly, came over and Tim offered them something in his hand. The dogs, saliva dripping from their jaws, licked the treat up and then sat panting as if asking for more.

I'll scream if they dribble that muck on me, she thought but she realised that the puppy on her lap had closed his eyes and his little chest was rising and falling as he slept. His body felt warm on her leg and very soft, much softer than she had imagined – and so far, no teeth or claws to worry about.

"All right?" asked Noah.

Holly nodded and then her phone pinged.

Struggling to check the message without waking her puppy, she saw that it was Jay. Reception was better out here. Two bars.

Just enough, she thought with relief.

jay: RUOK
holly: yep havent heard from U
jay: been busy
holly: oh

There was a pause and Holly wondered what to say. Jay had been so angry when she'd lost touch but she wasn't sure if she should be angry back. I'll wait and see if he explains, she decided.

jay is typing...

jay: U at home
holly: yep

No need to tell him I'm out with my friends, is there? she told herself.

jay: doing homework?
holly: not yet
jay: why not??
    : U got a friend there?
    : someone U rather be with
holly: no
    : anyway havent heard from you since this morning
jay: told you
    : been busy

: but if U dont believe me

: U rather be with UR mates

: ignore me

: im used 2 being on my own

Holly stared at the messages as they streamed down the screen. It's like he's mad at me but he's the one who was too busy to chat. She felt confused and a bit angry but also scared. I can't row with him. I just can't, she told herself.

"Everything OK?" asked Noah.

Looking up she saw his eyes were full of concern but a sliver of irritation shot through her.

She frowned and shook her head.

"Must be her boyfriend," said Ellen in a teasing voice.

"Shut up," snapped Holly but she noticed Noah staring at her and there was that pinched look creeping back into his face.

"All right, keep your hair on and mind that puppy." Ellen reached over and picked the tiny animal up, cradling it in her arms and making cooing noises.

"The puppy was all right," Holly growled, as Tim shot her one of his puzzled looks.

Her phone pinged twice. She stared at the screen. Jay was sulking at her and complaining about her friends.

"I've switched my phone off," muttered Ellen. "We always do up here, don't we Tim?"

Tim stood up, brushing of his school trousers and said in his calm manner, "Dad's got tea and cake for us."

Noah stood up too, looking brighter and said, "I'm starving."

They all took off and then Noah stopped and looked

round, "Coming Holly?"

Her phone was pinging and pinging and for a moment she didn't know where she wanted to be. These were her friends. But then she read Jay's latest messages.

jay: sorry happyholly
    : so lonely without U
    : felt jealous
    : UR with UR mates and mines dead

I have to be with Jay, she told herself. He needs me more than ever.

Noah was waiting, picking straw off his blazer. He suddenly looked so young, standing there in his school uniform, trouser legs flapping around his thin legs. My Jay is way more mature, she told herself.

"I'd better go, homework, you know."

Noah nodded, his head lowered. "OK. Will your mum be home?"

Holly snorted. "Doubt it. She's with Gran all the time these days."

"What about dinner?"

"Get my own. Pizza again." Holly stared at her screen and Noah, turned away, his shoulders drooping.

I've done so much for him this week, she told herself, feeling an impatient stab in her belly. What else does he want?

She took off down the side of the house and strode to the bus stop. She had to wait ten minutes and then she was on the bus, rolling back down the steep roads towards Brighton, messaging Jay all the way.

Chapter 16
First Date

The next morning Holly was stopped in the corridor by a furious Miss Holland.

"How dare you skip my detention yesterday," snapped the teacher, arms folded blocking Holly's way. "I don't recognise you these days, Holly Bennett. Do I need to tell your mother to come up and see me?"

"No," said Holly, horrified. She pulled the forged note out of her bag. "Sorry Miss, had a toothache yesterday afternoon and Mum made me an appointment to see the dentist after school."

The teacher took the note and read it with a frown. Then she gave a swift nod and said, "All right. But be there after school today, or else."

Holly breathed a sigh of relief as she watched the teacher stride away.

A triumphant feeling spread through her as she went into class. Got away with it! she thought and almost fist pumped the air.

* * *

It was too cold and damp at lunchtime to go outside and Holly didn't want to sit with the others to eat her sandwich. Prowling around the she found one of the tiny music practice rooms unlocked and sat down on a piano stool.

Now I can message Jay in private, she told herself with a happy sigh.

holly: having a cheese and cucumber sandwich
jay: me 2
   : how long till afternoon school?
holly: ten minutes
jay: wish we could chat all day
holly: me 2

"Holly?"

Holly's head jerked up and with relief she saw it was only Noah. What if Miss Holland caught her with her phone inside the building?

"What is it?" she muttered.

"Missed you at lunch. What're you doing in here?"

Holly waved her phone and in a sarcastic voice said, "Chatting. Is that OK with you?"

Noah's face closed down in that pinched look again but Holly rolled her eyes and went back to her phone as messages streamed in from Jay.

Why doesn't Noah just disappear? she thought with irritation. He winds me up these days. If I hadn't gone to Tim's yesterday then me and Jay could've messaged for so much longer. Each moment together is so precious.

"You're on the phone a lot these days, aren't you?" said Noah. "Ellen says you have a boyfriend. Is he in our school?"

Holly shrugged but didn't answer. If I keep quiet then Jay can't accuse me of blabbing about us and eventually Noah will get the message and scram, she told herself.

It took a super-human effort not to say Scram! out loud.

"OK. Better go." Noah turned to leave and then he hesitated.

What now? grumbled Holly to herself.

"I'm your friend, Holly. Whatever happens," said Noah and then he disappeared.

What on earth does he mean by that? thought Holly but she forgot all about it as her phone pinged.

jay: one week today
   : since we met
   : virtually i mean
holly: yep
jay: so glad i met U my beautiful holly
   : U changed my life
   : feel like ive know U for months
holly: me 2!!
jay: we have so much in common
   : never get bored chatting 2 U
holly: me 2 dont want to be with anyone else
    : not family
    : friends
    : amy
    : none of them get me like U
jay: same
   : UR the only one who understands me
   : always here for U babes
holly: me 2

jay: *sticker: *boy with huge red heart on his back saying
    I LOVE YOU*

There was a pause as Holly stared at the sticker, a hot glow running through her. Jay loves me, went round and round in her mind.

jay : UR my first girlfriend

Holly nearly jumped up and shouted YESSSS!! out loud but managed to stop herself in time. She didn't want to be discovered. The music rooms were out of bounds.

jay: RUOK
    : never had a girlfriend
holly: *three smiley emojis*
    : never had a boyfriend
jay: so we R the same
holly: of course!!!
jay : YESSSSS!!

The bell went for afternoon school and Holly was just about to shut her phone down when one more message came in.

jay: really wanna meet U
    : where do U live?
    : wanna meet up
    : cant wait any longer
    : how about it holly???
    : U can trust me

She could hear the corridor filling up with noisy chatter. Everyone was on their way to classes. If she stopped now to answer Jay a teacher could spot her.

Not worth the risk, she decided, putting her phone on silent and dropping it into her bag.

As she sat in Science with the computer boys whispering to each other, Holly stared into the blue flame of the Bunsen burner and asked herself over and over, Do I trust Jay enough to tell him where I live?

It was almost a no-brainer, as the Science teacher often said in a sarcastic voice.

Yes I do. A thrill poured through her as she made her decision. Now Jay will know how much I trust him.

And love him?

After school all she wanted to do was rush off and message Jay but first she had to endure a forty-minute detention in the PE block, cleaning out lockers, with Miss Holland glaring at her.

Finally she was free and she decided to take the bus to the beach. She didn't want to go home just yet. I want to be with Jay in my special place, she told herself.

The rain had stopped by the time she arrived and was walking down to the pier. The sky, whiter now, had cleared along the horizon, a ribbon of red gleaming as the sun set. There was a sharp smell of frost in the air.

Is it going to snow? Holly wondered, as she settled herself under the pier, took out her phone and messaged Jay.

holly: i live in Brighton
jay: OMG im a few miles away

holly: cant believe it

jay: i know

holly: i go 2 vintage shops in north laines

: cheaper than the lanes near the beach

jay: thats where i shop 2

holly: cant believe it

jay: me 2

: probably passed U in the street

: before i knew U of course

holly: im sure we did

: like millions of times

jay: zillions

: haha

holly: luv brighton

jay: YAAY!! me 2

holly: lots of students doing mad stuff

jay: yep awesome

holly: last week they went in the sea!!

: took off their jeans

: bit embarrassing

: * emoji: red face*

jay: sorry they upset U

: UR such a nice girl holly

: students are nutters!!

Holly laughed and looked up. How completely amazing that Jay lived near Brighton and loved it as much as she did. Unbelievable luck, she told herself. Does he like the pier too?

She took a selfie which showed iron girders behind her and then took a couple of pictures of the structure going out to sea. It was much colder now and the final glow of sunlight on the horizon had disappeared. A swell was rising and the water had turned a chilly grey.

But my new jacket's good, she told herself and Jay's love is keeping me warm.

Holly is typing...

holly: on the beach right now
    : under the pier
    : my fave place in the world
    :* two photos*
jay: OMG!!
    : dont believe it!!!
holly: what??
jay: me and mike always met under the pier
    : mike lived in brighton
    : it was our favourite place 2
holly: cant believe it
    : we have sooo much in common
jay: yep

There was a pause. Holly waited and then she saw Jay typing.

jay: wanna ask U something
holly: what?
jay: scared U will say no
holly: try me
jay: wanna meet U under the pier
    : saturday morning 9.30
    : thats where i wanna be 2 remember mike
    : on the anniversary of his death

Our first date, thought Holly with a thrill. And Jay needs me.

holly: i wanna be there with U 2
jay: AWESOME!!

It was getting dark and Holly went off to catch the bus home, messaging Jay all the way.

Wednesday night; Dad was away on business again and Mum had messaged her after school to say that Gran was feeling lonely and she was going over to spend the evening with her. There was another message about making it up to her on Saturday but Holly didn't even answer.

I'm with Jay on Saturday, she told herself as she let herself into the empty house. It's our first date and no way are Mum and Dad going to spoil things. Even if I have to sneak out of the house really early.

Which means I'll have to get up even earlier to get ready, she told herself. But she didn't care. Jay would do anything for me. And I'd do anything for him. That's what it means to have a boyfriend.

Madison had been talking about Harry this morning before the form teacher had arrived to take the register. The Bezzies were clustered at the back of the room and Holly wandered over to listen in. Becca Wilson was leaning against a cupboard, bony arms folded, head to one side, listening too. She had a sneer on her face.

"So Harry came over and helped me with that horrible Science homework and he has so much coursework you know, for his Law A Level." Madison looked round the adoring group as they muttered agreement.

Becca gave a snort but when Madison threw her a puzzled look, Becca was already staring at her nails.

Muppet, Holly told herself.

"Harry would do anything for me," Madison went on, tossing her gleaming blonde hair to one side and combing her fingers through it. "He's *such* a lovely boyfriend."

"You're so lucky," said one of the girls, with a longing sigh.

"He's the lucky one, if you ask me, you lot panting over every word about pretty-boy Harry," said Becca in her sharp voice.

Aisha put her wide shoulders back and said, "No-one's asking you, dumbo."

Yesss! thought Holly. Finally Aisha is useful for something.

She'd thought about Madison's words all day. What makes a good boyfriend/ girlfriend? she asked herself. Being there, whatever it takes, she decided.

But now, as she dumped her bag and went into the kitchen, she couldn't help remembering Noah's words before he left the music room, *I'm your friend, Holly. Whatever happens.*

She shrugged to herself. It's not the same as me and Jay.

She checked the oven out of habit but it was cold as usual. Putting up the temperature on the heating to the maximum, she ran upstairs and pulled on a T and shorts, pushing her feet into trainers. I'll pretend me and Jay are in Spain, she decided, as she ran downstairs again with a grin on her face.

Not feeling very hungry – it's *lurv*, she told herself, with a giggle – she poured some oven chips into a dish and threw them in the oven. Then she opened a huge bag of crisps and settled down at the kitchen table with her tablet and her phone.

As she chatted to Jay she watched one of Sandi's videos on the tablet about getting ready for a date.

"Start with the eyebrows," Sandi said, her dark eyes grinning at the screen, mouth pouting as she chattered on about dating.

Holly felt a thrill that she was planning her very first date with a boy.

"I'm putting champagne pink on my eyelids," said Sandi, simpering at the camera.

Love that colour, thought Holly, and made a note of it.

"Now, pink passion blush on my cheeks and rose pink on my lips. Finish it off with my favourite gloss and there!" Sandi tipped her head to one side and shook her long dark hair. "Make-up done, time to choose my outfit."

holly is typing...

holly: do U like pink
jay: luv it if U do
holly: pink blusher
jay: lip gloss??
holly: haha
    : boys not interested in makeup

jay: im interested in what UR interested in babes

jay is typing...

jay: got U a present
holly: squueee
     : what ?
jay: a surprise
    : give it 2 U on Saturday
holly: its only Wednesday
      : have to wait 3 whole days!!
      : cant wait that long!!!
jay: haha have 2 wait
holly: is it makeup??
jay: no guessing
holly: jewellery??
jay: my lips R sealed
holly: perfume
     : chocolates
     : flowers
jay: UR very bad holly
   : * 4 smiley emojis*
holly: PLEAAAASSSEE tell me
jay: no

Holly read back through the message stream, laughing out loud. Jay has bought me a present! Can't believe it. Should I get him one?

No, she decided. She was sure Sandi would say, Not on the first date.

Will we go on more than one date? she wondered. She shook herself. Of course we will. Me and Jay, we're totally solid. I'm crazy about him and he's...

There was shouting in the street, so loud she could hear it all the way back in the kitchen. Men's voices, really angry, were bellowing away at each other, becoming louder and louder until there was the crashing sound of glass breaking.

Beer bottles, she thought. Is there a fight?

She padded out of the kitchen and down the hall. Peering through the front door she could see three large shapes looming by the gate. She shrank back. Then a car screeched up and there were more rough, deep voices, shouting and swearing.

What's going on? she thought, as fear welled up inside her. What if they come into the garden or even bang on the front door?

She wanted to run back to the kitchen to get her phone but her legs wouldn't move. The voices raged on and then suddenly there was a massive thump at the back of the house. The living room door rocked on its creaky hinges.

OMG!! Someone's in the garden. Maybe they're trying to break in.

Panic rocketed through her. Without a second thought, Holly grabbed her jacket, shoved her feet into her trainers and wrenching open the front door, ran outside as the men jumped into a car, roared away and veered sharp left into the side street.

They're heading for the back of the house, she thought.

There was a service road which ran along the back, past the end of Holly's garden.

I have to get away!

She ran out of the garden, onto the street and swerved right, away from the car, her mind a jumble of terrified thoughts.

They might come back.

I can't be in the house if they do.

Where shall I go?

Why isn't Amy still over the road?

The temperature had dropped almost to freezing and wet sleet was now falling. Holly's legs were bare in her shorts and she had no socks on. Her laces were undone and her trainers began to slip and slide over the pavement as the sleet fell harder and harder.

There was a pub up ahead but if she pushed open the door the barman would yell at her to leave. Shall I say I'm being followed? she thought. She looked behind and all around. No-one else was in the street. They wouldn't believe her, would tell her to go home.

I can't do that, it's too dangerous and anyway, she realised, I've forgotten my keys. How stupid!

Pausing in the light from the pub windows she shuffled in her pockets for her phone to ring Mum.

NO!!

I've left it on the kitchen table. Haven't even got my purse.

Oh God! Now what?

In the end the café on the next road was still open and she found a two pound coin in her pocket. Shivering with cold, she bought a coffee and slumped down in a corner, sipping the hot liquid. It was ten minutes past nine.

I'm not going back until at least ten, she told herself, pulling her jacket more tightly around to try and warm up. Jay will be annoyed I forgot my phone.

But then he'll comfort me.

The thought spread a sliver of warmth through her as she watched the hands of the clock slowly creep towards ten.

Chapter 17
Cupcakes for Holly

"What do you mean, you just went to the shop? At this time of night! And it's almost snowing."

Holly had arrived back home and to her intense relief, Mum answered the door – even if she was moaning again.

With an irritated sigh, Holly pushed past into the hallway, peeled off her jacket and slung it on the coat peg by the door. "I wanted some chocolate," she muttered.

Walking home from the café she realised if she told Mum about the men in the street and how scared she was, then maybe Mum and Dad would stay in more and keep an eye on her.

I don't want that, she told herself. Me and Jay wouldn't have any privacy.

"You must have been out for a long time," Mum went on, her voice becoming more and more shrill. "I've been home for over twenty minutes. And why did you go out on a night like this in your shorts?"

Ignoring her, Holly went down to the kitchen to find her phone.

The house was so warm it made her feel sleepy especially after the terrified flight from the house and being stranded on the streets.

Mum followed and leaning up against the sink, she folded her arms, raised her eyebrows and said, "Well?"

"I met up with a friend who was in the shop too."

"Boy or girl?" said Mum in a suspicious tone. "Who was this friend? Were there any strange men hanging around, Holly? Tell me the truth."

"All the men were in the pub, Mum," said Holly in a sarcastic tone. "I saw a girl from school. Becca."

"I thought you said you didn't like her."

Holly shrugged.

"So you and this Becca, did you go in the pub? Did she suggest it? Is that the sort of girl she is and you just followed on."

Holly tipped her head to one side and stuck her lower lip out. "Do you honestly think they would serve me in the pub? I'm only fourteen."

"Don't speak to me in that tone!" Her mother dumped a couple of pans in the sink with a crash.

Holly jumped at the noise.

Then Mum said in a hoarse voice, "Dressed like that quite frankly you look like a little hussy."

Holly stared at her mother in horror. Is that what she thinks of me? What if Jay was here and he heard her talk to me like that?

Her cheeks flamed as a picture of her and Jay sitting on the sofa came into her mind, Jay's arm around her shoulders and Mum coming in and calling Holly a hussy.

From somewhere deep inside her a scream of rage

flew up and out of her mouth so loud she even surprised herself.

"So now I know what you *really* think of me!!" she yelled, ignoring the shocked look on her mother's face.

Grabbing her phone, tears welling in her eyes, Holly ran off.

She could hear Mum coming after her, heels tapping over the slate tiles. "No Holly, wait. You don't understand. I'm just worried about you, so's your Dad."

Holly was halfway up the stairs but she turned and glared down at Mum, standing at the bottom, her arms hanging loose by her side, eyes wide.

"*You're* the one who doesn't understand," she cried out. Then she ran up to her room and slammed the door as hard as she could.

Holly threw herself on her bed and began reading Jay's messages asking where she was. He's going to be so angry with me, she told herself.

She crawled under the duvet, shivering, her clothes feeling damp and chill and started to message the whole story.

    holly: but i forgot my key
        : couldnt go home
        : had to sit in a café until mum came back
        : so sorry jay didnt stop thinking about U
        : how U wanna chat about mike an everything
        : really really sorry

    jay is typing

    jay: babes its OK

: i understand an wish i was there 2 keep U safe
: so worried about U

Holly stared at the phone with relief. He isn't angry with me, he understands and he's sorry for me, she thought. A warm rush of love spread through her. He's the only one who really cares about me, she told herself.

holly: mum was angry i went out in the dark
jay: yep
holly: she was horrible
jay: what did she do?
holly: shouted at me and asked if i went to the pub
    : would never do that!!
jay: course not!! UR a nice girl
   : she shouldnt say that
holly: she said something much worse
jay: what??
holly: she called me a hussy
jay: BABES!! So harsh!!
   : U must be angry
   : IM ANGRY!!!
   : UR mum should never say that
   : UR such a nice sweet beautiful lovely girl
   : trust me i know U better than anyone
   : UR not a hussy babes
   : listen to me
   : jay knows best

Jay's words poured on down the screen, soothing her until her eyes were closing and she fell asleep still holding her phone in her hand.

When she woke up, bleary eyed and still in her clothes from last night, she could hear the radio blaring in the kitchen downstairs.

Mum's down there she thought. I can't face another row.

She crept out to the bathroom and then went back to pull on her uniform and grab her bag. Sneaking downstairs she took her jacket from the peg, checked she had her keys and purse and slipped out of the house. Her stomach was rumbling. She'd hardly eaten anything the day before.

Bacon sandwich at the station café, she decided. It was only a short walk from the station to school and she had plenty of time.

The bus went all the way to the station and once Holly had bought her sandwich and a coffee, she settled down to send Jay snaps of her breakfast. He sent her a snap of himself standing in a street she didn't recognise – but he doesn't live in Brighton she reminded herself – and another of a large takeaway coffee.

> jay: breakfast together
> holly: perfect
> jay: wanna take you somewhere special on saturday
> holly: what about remembering mike
> jay: course got that all planned
>   : gonna read a poem and everything
> holly: thats so lovely jay
> jay: he was my best mate
>   : but we could go somewhere after
> holly: awesome

jay: do U have a fave caff??

Holly paused at the word caff. Mum would have said that's common and then Dad would have rolled his eyes.

Why didn't Jay write café?

Don't be stupid, she thought and who cares what Mum thinks? She can be such a snob.

jay: U there?
holly: yep
    : theres a nice place called hotcakes in the lanes
jay: if U like it then i like it
holly: they make the best cupcakes in brighton
    : * photo of a chocolate cupcake *
jay: mmmmm!!!
   : LUV choc cupcakes
   : sweet cupcakes for my holly

Holly felt a warm glow spread through her. Only Jay can make me feel like this, she thought. Mum and Dad just made her angry these days. She was certain Mum would have rung Dad last night and moaned on and on about Holly running around the streets like a hussy.

To think I was looking forward to taking Jay home to meet them, she told herself as she walked to school, messaging. I must have been insane. They are NEVER going to meet my Jay.

It was dry enough and not too cold at lunchtime to take her sandwich outside. She settled down on a bench to message Jay. She was grinning at a silly sticker he'd sent over when a shadow fell across her screen.

Looking up she saw Madison and Aisha.

"Definitely in love," said Aisha.

"Told you," said Madison, in a teasing voice. "Let's see a pic, Holly. Is he as fit as my Harry."

Holly nearly clicked on a photo of Jay then, she felt so desperate to show him off. But Jay's voice was in her head: we R private holly: we R special.

Her face flushing, Holly gave a shrug and raised her eyebrows.

"Aw, she's embarrassed," said Madison, rolling her eyes at Aisha. "Message me, sweetheart, if you want any tips for your first date."

"Yeah, like, don't go too far the first time?" sneered Aisha.

Madison play-punched her arm. "Holly's not like that. Just ignore her," she said, shaking her head at Holly.

Holly smiled, not knowing what to say. Don't give anything away, she told herself.

They moved off which was a relief but then she saw Ellen and Tim coming over, holding hands.

Now what? she thought, with an inward sigh. Can't I have any peace and quiet to be with my Jay?

"All right?" said Tim in his friendly voice, earphones hanging loose around his neck.

Tim was wearing his black wool hat pulled low and Ellen was wearing a smaller one with a peak, her long hair flowing out around her head.

They looked so comfortable together, Holly thought with a jealous pang.

In some ways they were so much more mature than Madison and the Bezzies. It felt like Madison couldn't have a boyfriend without the Bezzies admiring everything she said.

Stupid really, Holly told herself.

Ellen and Tim knew how to *be* together without making any fuss.

She gave an inward sigh. Still two whole days before Saturday and her very first date with Jay.

A rush of impatience went up through her and she glared up at Tim.

He stared back, eyebrows furrowed and then looked at Ellen as if for support.

"Got all your important stuff done last night, then?" said Ellen in a cold voice.

"What's it to you?" snapped Holly. Maybe Ellen hadn't changed all that much, she thought. Still knows how to be mean.

Tim shot them both a puzzled look and gave his nervous little cough.

"Let's go," growled Ellen. "She obviously hasn't got time for her real friends."

Ellen pulled Tim's hand but as they walked away, his puzzled look seemed to say, What's going on Holly?

She felt a pang of sadness inside. She had to admit it was nice having friends in school again. She didn't want to give up her place on the lunch table. What if it started raining again and she had to sit indoors?

Maybe once me and Jay are dating properly, we could go out as a foursome, she thought. We could ask Noah to join us so he doesn't feel left out.

Feeling generous, Holly went back to her phone.

When she raised her eyes again, Noah had joined Tim and Ellen. They were all standing a short distance away and it seemed to Holly they were taking it in turns to stare towards her; Tim still looking puzzled, Noah with that pinched look and Ellen giving one of her evil stares.

Holly's phone pinged and she looked away with relief.

jay: go straight home tonight holly
   : dont go out in the dark
   : message me i will keep you safe
holly: yep promise
    : no more wandering the streets
jay: without your keys!!
holly: yep haha
jay: friday tomorrow and then saturday
   : finally get to meet U
   : YAAY!!
holly: two more sleeps
    : feels like weeks!!
jay: I know
   : mad aint it??
holly: feels like ive know U for months
jay: same 4 me
   : going home to wrap UR present after school
holly: sooo exciting
jay: *sticker: boy's face surrounded by slogan, GOT YOU ON MY MIND*
   : *sticker: boy saying, LUV YA*

Holly searched through all the stickers, swiping her screen like mad until she found the one she wanted.

holly: *sticker: Girl carrying a red heart on her back
      saying, I LOVE YOU MORE*
jay: AWESOME!!!

There was another pause while Jay typed and then a photo came in.

jay: * photo: chest bare, black swim shorts, bare legs and
      feet, eyes squinting in bright sunshine*

A stab of fear went through Holly. Why did he send that? It reminded her straight away about the disgusting snap jimmycoolguy had sent her and how he wanted one back only in her underwear.

Is Jay going to ask me to send a pic without my top on?

Her mind ached with worry as she watched the screen.

Jay was typing.

If he asks me anything I don't like, what should I do? she thought. Dump him?

Oh God! The thought sent a shudder through her. I couldn't bear it, she told herself.

jay: RUOK
holly: yep
jay: did you like the photo?
    : holiday in spain with mike and his family

Holly went weak with relief. It was just an innocent holiday snap. Jay had been with his best friend and their family. He wasn't sending her – well – sexy pictures let alone demanding anything back.

> holly: nice
> jay: yep we had such a great time
>   : hey U gone a bit quiet
>   : was it OK sending that pic??
> holly: yep
> jay: should have sent one with my T on
>   : holly??
>   : sorry if U didn't like it
> holly: i did but
>   : not sending one back in my swim stuff
> jay: NOO!! course not
>   : wouldnt ask you babes
>   : STUPID ME!!
>   : should never have sent it

Jay's apologies streamed down the screen, soothing Holly's fears and then someone was standing over her. Looking up she saw Becca Wilson with a sneer on her face. Another girl was standing with her.

Kelly E, thought Holly, with a sinking feeling. There were three Kellys in her year but Kelly E was one of the worst girls in school. She and Amy avoided her like the plague.

Kelly E was very thin but taller than Holly, with straggly hair which hung over her face. She'd been suspended more than once and thought nothing of punching anyone who annoyed her; boys or girls.

Amy said that Kelly's parents were never around and her big brothers – who were often in trouble with the police – were the ones who looked after her.

"Not doing a very good job, are they?" Amy would say and they'd roll their eyes at each other.

Now as the girls stood over her, sniggering to each other, Becca suddenly reached out and snatched Holly's phone. "Who're you chatting to so much?" she asked, curling up her lip.

Kelly gave a snort, chewing an end of her hair.

"Give it back!" snarled Holly, leaping to her feet but Becca was too quick for her.

Swiping the screen, Becca said, "Oh, still Jay, is it?" She read out in a mocking voice, "I've been stupid/ forgive me babes." Becca sniggered again and then she said, "You had a date yet? Bet he's a manky kisser."

"It's none of your business," said Holly. "Give me back my phone."

"Mmm, nice pic," said Becca.

She showed Kelly and for a second the other girl's hair was blown back from her face and Holly saw a flash of something – fear? worry? – on Kelly's face.

Does she know my Jay as well? she thought, with a sinking feeling.

Becca held out the phone and Holly grabbed it back, her face hot as an electric plate.

The two girls moved off and Holly sat back down again, fuming to herself. She's always been after my Jay, she thought and now Kelly E is around too. No way would Jay be interested in *her*. Would he?

But then she heard what sounded like Jay's name floating across the playground.

Her head jerked up to see Becca and Kelly stop near Tim, Ellen and Noah. Becca was laughing out loud, her head thrown back and then she spun round on her heels and stared straight at Holly.

It felt like the whole Year was gossiping about her.

Ellen had said they were her 'real' friends.

What sort of friends gossip about you behind your back? she asked herself.

And what's Becca up to now? A spear of anger ran up through her.

Is she jealous about me and Jay?

Well, she can just get over it.

Jay's mine.

Forever.

Chapter 18
Another Photo

Holly's phone pinged. It was Amy.

amy: hey holly
: whats new??

It was Friday lunchtime and Holly was sitting outside on the bench that used to be hers and Amy's. Her eyes were almost closing, she was so tired. She'd messaged with Jay most of the night.

As Saturday morning crept closer, she didn't know who was more impatient to meet up; her or Jay. It gave her such a delicious feeling every time he said he could hardly wait to see her in the real.

Now as she read Amy's message, Jay's warning words came in her ear: must be a slow time: thats why shes messaging U: she doesn't really care about U.

I'll keep it short, Holly told herself.

But she couldn't help feeling a bit pleased, especially as she didn't feel much like hanging with the others in the past couple of days.

holly: nothing much
amy: minus ten degrees today!!
　: snow really deep
　: we get tons more out here than the cities
　: fed up with snow!!!
　: getting boring now
　: mum keeps saying its nearly spring in england
　: she misses her garden
holly: thought you loved all that snow and skiing and stuff
amy: you cant ski every day
　: so gimme the gossip
　: madison and the bezzies still a crew??
　: and whats becca up to?

Holly frowned at the screen. Why's she asking about Becca? Has Becca mentioned me and Jay? But Holly was sure the other girl had no idea about the first date tomorrow.

holly: dunno ok i suppose
amy: who do you hang with?
holly: whoever
amy: me and gabe broke up
　: he said he wanted his freedom!!
　: honestly holly i really dont get dating
　: missing U sooo much

Oh yeah? thought Holly. Jay's right. She's broken up with her stupid boyfriend and she's bored, so she messages me. She thinks I don't have any friends and

I'm sitting around waiting for her to get in touch.

Furious, Holly stabbed at the keys.

holly   : gotta go lesson time
amy: oh shame message later???
               : wish U were here
               : no one like U in my school

I don't believe a word, thought Holly. Not after all those sleepover pics. And I bet she's still with that Gabe. Probably they had a row, she told herself and Amy doesn't want to admit it to her Canadian friends. So she messages good old boring, safe Holly. That's how she sees me – three thousand miles away!

It was time for class and as she walked back across the field, eyes glued to the screen, a voice said in her ear, "Seen Tim?"

Looking up she saw Ellen and her blue eyes were fixed on Holly. Her face had lost the mean look from the previous day which was a relief.

"No," Holly said in a neutral voice.

Ellen fell into step beside her, saying, "You OK? Sorry if I was a bit horrible yesterday. It's just we thought you'd gone off from Tim's in a bit of a mood."

Holly shrugged, "Yep, no… I was just a bit busy."

"OK." Ellen opened her hand and sitting in the palm was an enamel brooch of a cat, in deep purple and red. "Tim gave it to me," she said, a smile on her face which was lit for a moment in a ray of winter sunlight.

Holly nodded. "Really pretty." Then almost without thinking, she blurted out, "Actually I'm meeting my boyfriend on the beach tomorrow morning, under the pier. He wants to take me out somewhere."

"Nice," said Ellen and then spotting Tim up ahead, she called out and ran off to meet him.

I shouldn't have told her, thought Holly, with a worried sigh. Jay would be furious. But then she told herself, I can introduce him to everyone after tomorrow.

The worried feelings subsided as she thought how that would show Becca and her horrible mate, Kelly.

But as she followed the crowd towards the outside door, she couldn't help wondering why Kelly was giving her such strange looks the day before when Becca was teasing her about Jay. Almost as though she was scared of something.

But no, Kelly E wasn't afraid of anything. She was just bad through and through.

Holly was about to turn her phone off before going inside when there was a ping. No message but Jay had sent over a photo.

Holly stared at the screen. She saw a boy with fair hair, shaved short and tanned skin, wearing only small, tight, navy blue swim trunks – the ones that look like pants, she couldn't help thinking. Not like those swimming shorts the boys wore these days.

It gave her a creepy feeling.

The boy had his arm around a girl wearing a tiny bikini – hardly covering her at all, thought Holly. I'd never wear anything like that and nor would Mum.

The girl had slipped the strap off one shoulder. They both had very long bare legs and were standing on a beach in blazing sunshine. The girl had her mouth in a pout as if kissing the air and the boy's head was turned towards her, grinning.

The phone felt hot in her hand and as the others pushed around her towards school, Holly knew she had to switch off and get to class before she was in trouble again.

Who are these two? rumbled through her head as she walked off. Friends of Jay? Why's he sent me a photo like that?

All afternoon as she sat in History and then French, all she could think about was the photo – it made her feel so uncomfortable, even a bit scared – puzzling over and over in her mind why Jay would send her such a photo.

What does he want? she wondered.

Between lessons she managed to slip into a quiet room and message Jay.

holly: got the pic
    : who is it??

But there was no answer and then she had to switch off and run to class.

After school, walking swiftly down the road to avoid Noah and the others, there was still no message from Jay. All the way home she stared at her screen, scrolling up to look at the photo again.

holly: RU there
    : whos in that pic??

There was no answer by the time she arrived home.

To her surprise both Mum and Dad were in the kitchen. The heating was on and there was a delicious smell coming from the oven.

"Family dinner, darling," called out Mum, a cloth over her shoulder. "Dad's back from his trip."

"Haven't seen you all week, Hol Pol," said Dad coming over to give her a kiss on the cheek. "What you been up to?"

His face was lit with his warm comfortable grin and Holly smiled back. The kiss felt good on her skin. For a moment she thought, Shall I show them the pic of Jay on the beach and the new photo? Tell Mum and Dad these are my friends, this is what I'm up to now and I'm not bothered you're too busy for me.

She stopped herself in time. She knew deep inside that they wouldn't like the photos, especially the one of the strange boy and girl. If she was honest, it was a very – well – sexy picture and she didn't like it much herself.

If Mum and Dad saw those photos there'd be loads of boring questions. They might make her go and spend the weekend with them at Gran's. No signal and no meeting Jay on the beach in the morning.

So she said in a normal voice, "What's for dinner?"

"Beef stew and dumplings, chocolate cake and ice cream," said Mum with a pleased look on her face.

Holly gave a nod and forced a smile on her face. "Yummy. I'll just go and get changed."

As she walked out of the kitchen she overheard Dad say to Mum, "Can't see why you're worried. She seems the same to me."

Mum said something back but Holly couldn't hear it. She went upstairs, wondering what Mum had been saying to Dad but relieved he didn't sound angry or anything.

I need Dad on my side tonight, she told herself. To keep Mum off my back.

As she was changing her phone pinged.
Jay!
At last, she thought, swiping the screen.

jay: RUOK
   : phone died
   : had to get it fixed in the shop
   : all good now
holly: OK
jay: did U like the pic of mike?
   : only one ive got
   : with his sister in spain

Holly felt her knees go weak with relief and she collapsed onto the bed. Jay wasn't sending her rude photos. Of COURSE he wasn't. It was just a pic of Mike with his SISTER!!

She almost whooped aloud with joy.

holly: didnt realise it was mike
jay: oh forgot to tell you
holly: OK
jay: nice pic isnt it?
   : mike and his sister together
holly: yep

Jay's explained, so why do I still have a weird feeling

inside, Holly wondered. Because he hasn't sent loads of messages apologising and asking if I'm OK, like he usually does. Tonight he's – well – brushing it over.

But then she shook herself. Isn't that what you want, Holly? A mature boyfriend. You're not a baby who needs to be comforted all the time. It's Madison who likes to be treated like a doll.

jay is typing ...

jay: we have all night now
holly: family dinner first
jay: cant U say U have homework
holly: not good idea
    : have 2 keep them sweet
    : so they dont make me go 2 gran this weekend again
jay: *sticker: boy looking miserable saying D'OH*
holly: *sad emoji*
jay: make an excuse 2 get away early
    : say UR tired or feeling sick or something
holly: could do
    : will try my best
jay: course U will
    : cant wait 2 see UR face when i give U my present
holly: soo exciting
    : ages till tomorrow morning
jay: I KNOW!!!
holly: can show U my new jacket
jay: cool

Holly started to pick out a nice top to wear for dinner as she messaged Jay but checking in the mirror she decided it would be better to stick to an old T. She didn't want to alert Mum and Dad to anything unusual this evening.

holly: going to dinner now
        : laters
jay: *sticker: boy with tears pouring saying WAAH*
    : *sticker: boy sitting on a seesaw alone saying MISS U
      SO MUCH*
holly: wont be long promise
jay: so lonely
holly: *sad emoji*

She went out of her room and downstairs trying to decide what she could say to get away early. Jay really needs me tonight, she told herself.

The table was already laid and Dad was sitting in his place.

"Not dressing up for me tonight, Hol?" he said grinning when she came in.

Holly shrugged and sat down, putting her phone by her plate.

It pinged twice.

"Sound off, please," called out Mum.

Holly frowned and pressed mute but she read Jay's messages and tapped a couple of replies.

Mum dished up and Holly settled down to eat her first proper meal for days. She was sick of pizza and chips.

Mum and Dad chatted about work stuff for a while as Holly ate, eyes glued to her phone.

Then Mum said in an irritated voice, "For goodness' sake, Holly. Switch that thing off while we eat. It's impossible to get your attention these days."

Holly looked up surprised. Mum was frowning and even Dad was giving her a puzzled stare.

Her immediate thought was to stick out her lower lip and snap back. Just in time she stopped herself. I don't want a row tonight, she thought.

Giving a small sigh, she switched the phone off and said to Mum, "Satisfied?"

Mum opened her mouth to reply but Dad cut in, "We need to talk about tomorrow, Hol Pol."

Holly scraped up the last of her stew and said, "What about tomorrow?"

"We're taking Gran to see Auntie May," said Dad.

Auntie May was Gran's older sister. She was nearly eighty and lived in a Home for old people more than two hours' drive away.

Holly nodded and said, "That's nice. You could take them both out to lunch somewhere – um – nice."

"We're all going," said Mum in a firm voice. "You need to be ready by nine. We have to pick up Gran and then drive to Auntie May and they both like to have lunch by twelve thirty." Mum gave an irritated sigh.

Dad rolled his eyes at Holly who stared back.

She was thinking hard. No point yelling and slamming doors, she told herself as she felt a rage rising inside. I have to be careful or no Jay and no beach in the morning. She thought longingly of her present. She was so excited to see what Jay had bought her.

No way am I going to miss our first date.

"OK," she said, playing for time.

I need a little white lie, she thought, and then it came to her.

Both her parents were staring at her. Dad laid his knife and fork carefully on his empty plate.

"The problem is," Holly said in a calm voice, "I have a massive maths test next week and you know how weak I am on algebra. I spent ages with the Maths teacher at lunchtime yesterday," – genius, she thought, amazed at how easily she lied these days – "and he gave me all this extra stuff to help me revise. I must study tomorrow."

Before Mum could snap back an answer, Holly played her trump card. "If I fail this test, the Maths teacher said I would probably be moved down to a lower group. That would be so humiliating, I couldn't bear it."

Mum closed her mouth and Dad reached out and patted her on the hand saying, "Don't worry, angel. I'm sure that won't happen. But in the circumstances," he raised an eye at Mum who glared back. "I think you should stay home tomorrow. You can see Auntie May another time."

Holly forced a grin and nodded. Have I got away with it? she wondered.

Then Mum launched into one of her rants. "She can't possibly stay at home all day. Think about it! The silly girl was locked out of the house on Wednesday night because she was so thoughtless. We won't be home until after dark, anything could go wrong..." Mum managed to speak for over a minute without pausing for breath.

Holly and Dad rolled their eyes at each other – twice.

Holly waited patiently and when there was a pause she said in the same calm voice, "I've been at home alone loads of times in the dark because of Gran's Crisis. I'm old enough when it suits you. Well, I'm nearly fifteen now and I'll be fine."

Before Mum could snap back Dad put up his hand, palm out and said, "Holly's right – not about being nearly fifteen – time enough to get older, Hol Pol – but she's had to cope while we've been out in the evenings and I think she's been very sensible on the whole. Wednesday night was a one-off, right Hol?"

Holly gave a firm nod back.

"I'm happy for her to stay at home this time," Dad said.

He fixed Mum with a hard stare, eyebrows raised.

Mum gave a sigh and gathered up some plates.

Holly waited, breath held, wondering if Jay was sending lots of messages.

Then Mum said, "You have to stick at your homework and nothing else."

"Yes, of course."

"And I don't want you wandering the streets after dark, my girl."

"No Mum, promise."

"I've given a spare key to Linda Levy now. So if you ever get locked out again, you go straight round there and stay with Noah until we're home. Right!"

"Of course. Good idea, Mum."

There was a pause as Mum stared at Dad and Holly.

Then with a relenting nod, she said, "All right. You can stay at home tomorrow. There's stew left over for your dinner and you can make yourself a sandwich for lunch."

Holly nearly threw her arms around Mum's neck but held back in case she got suspicious.

Instead she gave Dad a meaningful stare and said in her most mature voice, "Lovely. Thanks Mum. And please give my love to Gran and Auntie May and say I'm sorry I couldn't come too."

Mum gave an approving nod. "That's very grown up of you darling. Let's hope all that silly behaviour we've seen lately is over and done with."

"Sorry, Mum," muttered Holly in a meek tone. "All right if I go up now? Get my books sorted out for the morning."

Mum gave a brief nod and Holly picked up her phone, pressing the side button to ON as she walked upstairs. Messages were streaming in as she went into the bedroom and threw herself onto her bed with relief.

All clear for tomorrow and now me and Jay can message all night.

Chapter 19
Meeting at Last

Holly made sure she was downstairs on Saturday morning by eight thirty for breakfast, showered and dressed.

Dad was in his usual chirpy mood, whistling a Beatles tune as toast jumped out of the toaster and into his hands. It was an old joke between him and Holly – toast has springs in our house – and today Holly played along, making Dad laugh as much as possible.

Mum dished up boiled eggs and Holly forced herself to eat but her tummy was fizzing with a mixture of excitement and nerves. She could hardly swallow.

As the kitchen clock edged towards nine Holly said, "I'll load the dish washer, Mum. You and Dad get ready to go. Long journey ahead."

"Thanks, darling," said Mum. "I've left a ten pound note on the hall table for emergencies. The phone signal isn't good in Auntie May's area; time they did something about that mast." Mum was checking her handbag. "I'll ring you once we're back on the road. Let you know what time we'll be home."

"Great," said Holly, scraping plates into the bin, trying to look mature and trustworthy.

"Study hard," said Dad with a grin, as he walked out the door.

"I will," Holly called back in a cheery voice.

Once they were gone Holly raced upstairs to put on her best top and jeans and then sat down in the front of the mirror to do her make-up.

Am I pretty? she thought, staring at her reflection, once she'd finished.

UR beautiful came Jay's words in her head.

Heart thumping, worried she'd be late, she threw a last glance in the mirror, went out of her room and downstairs.

Taking her new jacket from the hall peg she put it on, went out of the door and locked it behind her. A bus appeared at the top of the road. Breaking into a sprint, she reached the stop in time, jumped on and swiped her pass. It was twelve minutes past nine. Jay had been messaging her most of the night and for the past hour.

Is he more excited than me? she thought.

She almost wished Madison would get on the bus and she could tell her she was meeting her boyfriend. She was pretty sure Ellen had told Noah and Tim yesterday. Won't be long before everyone knows about me and Jay.

The thought sent a delicious feeling running through her.

As Holly arrived at the beach, a weak sun appeared between light grey clouds. It was cold enough to keep her jacket fastened. The water was a wintry grey but it was the end of February, the evenings were getting lighter and soon she and Jay would be able to go for long walks on the beach, hand in hand, imagining they were on that beach in Spain in Jay's photos.

She could see the pier now and she stopped for a moment at the top of the steps. Will he be there? Will I recognise him? People don't always look the same as their photos.

She felt a sudden rush of nerves. There were very few people around. A sea mist hung on the horizon and a fog horn sounded its long mournful tone in the distance.

A warning to ships, she thought, and shivered, putting her hands in her pockets to warm them. There was a plastic spoon discarded by the wall and it made her think of her collection. Hard to believe it was only two weeks ago today that she'd ended up at the shops, desperate to leave the house and all those spooky creaks. She could never have imagined that only four days later – Wednesday night – Jay would message her and now they were actually going on a proper date.

Taking her hands out of her pockets she skipped down the steps and crunched over the pebbles to the pier.

Standing under the iron girders, shadowed by the gloomy light cast under the huge structure, was – well – a man.

She creased up her eyes to see more clearly.

The man had his back to her. He was wearing a black hoody with the hood up and black jeans. His feet were in Converse trainers and his hands were shoved in his pockets, shoulders hunched against the cold. The man was a bit shorter than Dad and a slimmer build.

Where's my Jay? thought Holly.

Then the man turned and Holly stared and stared as the man pushed the hood off his head.

The light under the pier was dim but she could see a narrow face with a pointed chin; not how Holly had pictured Jay from the photo. But sort of similar, she thought. The man had light brown hair cut short and his skin was quite pale. It was clear he was already shaving.

Do boys shave at fourteen? she wondered.

As Holly adjusted to the light, she could see the wide hazel eyes and long lashes from the photo Jay had sent.

He looks likes my Jay, she thought, but older. I don't understand.

The man's face broke into a smile which hovered mainly around the mouth and he said, "Holly. It's me, Jay. Don't you recognise me, babes?"

Keeping his hands in his pockets he moved towards her.

Uncertain, Holly took a step back and nearly lost her footing.

"Whoah, babes." The man put out a hand and laid it on her arm to steady her. A warmth seeped through her jacket and he wasn't gripping hard.

It felt good, if she was honest.

"You're Jay?" asked Holly.

"Yes, it's me," said the man, in a low tone. "Am I a bit older than you thought?"

Holly nodded and glanced over her shoulder. No-one else was on this part of the beach. Should I be alone with him? she wondered.

"Just hear me out, Holly, please."

The man was fixing her with those hazel eyes and

they were so soft, like his voice, which she had to admit was very gentle. He wasn't trying to scare her.

She'd waited so long for this moment. She couldn't bear to walk away now.

"OK," she said.

The man started to speak in a husky voice. "I'm actually nineteen. A few years older than you, I know," said the man as Holly's eyebrows shot up. "But not that much older, Holly. Anyway you're dead mature. I can see that. We had a real connection the minute we started messaging, didn't we, babes? I fell in love with you. I couldn't help it. I'm so happy we've finally met up, babes."

The man stopped talking and put his hands back in his pockets.

Holly paused, taking all this in. Is this really my Jay? she wondered. Then she remembered the photo. "Whose photo did you send me?"

"My brother," said the man. "He's fifteen."

"So why not send a photo of you?"

"I was scared you'd think I looked too old or something. I didn't want to stop messaging you."

Holly's mind was bouncing from fact to fact, trying to anchor what was real and what was – well – made up? Lies?

No! she thought. My Jay wouldn't lie to me.

"I'm Jay, I really am Holly, I'm not that much older. Lots of girls your age go out with older guys, don't they?"

Holly thought of Madison's Harry who was sixteen. Not so much different from nineteen, was it?

The more the man talked – she began to think of him now as Jay – the more she could hear his voice from all the messages.

That's the way my Jay would speak, she told herself.

"And Mike? Is he real? Did he really die?"

"Yeah, course. Mike died last year and today's the anniversary."

"So why isn't his sister here?"

"Wanted to remember him in my own way. We were best mates, you know."

Holly paused for a moment and then she said, "So he was eighteen when he died?'

Jay shrugged and gave a little snicker. "Yeah. Course. We did everything together."

"Like what?"

"Like music. I work in a student bar and DJ for parties. Mike worked on the sets with me. It's really hard now he's… you know… passed."

He fixed his wide eyes on Holly and there was an awkward silence.

Then Jay said, "Got your present, babes."

He walked over to a backpack lying under the pier. Holly followed him and watched as he pulled out a beautifully wrapped package. He offered it to her.

Holly hesitated but her heart gave a little jump.

He really is my Jay, she told herself. He sounds like Jay, he really is missing Mike. He's five years older than me – well not quite five as I'll be fifteen in eleven months. But he's exactly like my lovely, sweet, kind, thoughtful Jay.

She reached out and took the package. "Thank you," she said, with a cautious smile.

She carefully removed the paper. Inside was a box of perfume.

"Wow!" she said. It was a very expensive brand.

Wait until I show Madison, zipped through her mind. Her stupid Harry never gave her anything like this.

"You're so worth it, babes," Jay said, tipping his head from side to side and stretching out his neck.

Cute, she thought.

"I'm crazy about you," Jay was saying. "You've been there for me when I've been thinking about Mike so much and I was lonely at home…"

"…but you're a bit old to miss your mum when she goes out and anyway, isn't your brother there?" she couldn't help saying.

It seemed to Holly that Jay's eyes narrowed and his jaw clamped into a hard line. But only for a second, as he smiled again with his mouth and said, "I know it sounds stupid, like really stupid, but I hate being home alone. I'm like you; I imagine every sound is a burglar breaking in. My brother often stays over with a mate."

As he spoke, Jay moved closer to Holly until he was just a few centimetres away, his eyes staring into hers. She felt as if she could sink into that soft hazel glow. She could smell a mixture of mint and a scent, probably his aftershave, which lingered in the air.

Putting his hands lightly on her shoulders he lowered his head and put his lips on hers.

We're kissing! she thought and it was wonderful. She felt as if she was floating on air.

He really loves me and I love him. Who cares about the age thing? I'm not bothered.

Holly closed her eyes and all she could hear was the sound of the sea breaking over the beach. Jay's lips were soft and minty on her mouth and his hands sent warm waves down her arms.

Then Jay moved away – Holly was sure she could stay like this forever – and picking up his pack, he walked further under the pier where the shadows were deeper and sat down on the beach, patting the pebbles.

Holly sat down next to him and Jay moved closer until their shoulders and sides were touching. It felt so warm and – well – right. She'd never sat this close to a boy before.

Jay pulled two cans of lager out of his pack, popped them both and handed one to her as if they did this all the time.

Holly took the can. She'd never been given an alcoholic drink before. Sometimes in the summer Dad made them shandy but it was mostly lemonade for Holly, with only a 'splash' of lager, as Dad always said.

Jay took a long drink from his can and then wiping his mouth with the back of his hand, he lit a cigarette, took a drag and handed it to Holly.

She hesitated and then took it and lifted it to her mouth.

"That lipstick really suits you, babe. You're so gorgeous, even more beautiful than your photo," he said in his husky voice.

Holly felt a thrill go through her. He might be older – could probably have any girl he wanted, she thought, he's so sweet and lovely – but it's me he wants to be with.

Glowing inside, she sucked cautiously on the cigarette and managed to blow the smoke out without coughing. She passed it back to Jay who took a couple of long drags.

It felt so grown up sitting under the pier with her – older – boyfriend, drinking and smoking, as if this was what they did every weekend.

"You're a star, Holly. A real star. No-one would ever know you were only fourteen," said Jay. "You look eighteen in that jacket, easy and what a pretty top. You're so gorgeous. I'm so lucky."

Holly felt as if she was basking in the sun as Jay talked.

"Had enough?" said Jay, draining his can and nodding to hers.

"Yep," said Holly.

Jay took it and stood the two cans under the pier, stubbing the cigarette out in one. It made quite a mess and normally she would hate anyone who left litter.

But today she couldn't care less.

Jay stood up and grabbing her hand helped her to her feet, like a proper gentleman.

Like Noah letting me go first onto the bus, she thought.

"Let's go, babes, lots to show you," said Jay.

"The café?" said Holly.

What else had Jay planned? A bubble of excitement rising inside her.

"Yeah, yeah, sure and…"

Before he could finish someone came flying under the pier, shouting, "No Holly! Don't go with him!"

Noah?!

What's he doing here?

Confused Holly took a step back as Noah came up to her side, yelling, "Run, Holly! Come on! Quick!"

Noah gripped her arm and yanked on it, a look of

terror on his face. She staggered and tripped forward, grabbing one of the girders to steady herself.

Before she could say anything, Jay rounded on Noah, looming over him, his face contorted with anger. "Get away from my girl, you nutter!! Go on, push off!"

"No, wait, Jay," she said, putting a hand forward to stop him. From what? she thought. Hitting Noah?

Noah took a step backwards. Jay had bunched his fists and he was so much bigger than the younger boy.

"Who is this creep?" snarled Jay. "Not having anyone messing with my girl?"

He's just protecting me, thought Holly. Noah's such an idiot. "It's... it's OK, Jay. He's... he's just a boy from my school," she stammered in a hoarse voice.

Turning to Noah, she snapped, "Why are you here? What's the *matter* with you?"

"I... I..." Noah started.

But Jay cut him off, barking out, "Yeah. What you doing here? Get off my beach before I make you. She's my girl. Not yours. Got it?"

Then without warning he threw a punch towards Noah's face. It didn't connect – of course not, thought Holly. He's just spooked by Noah. He wouldn't hurt him, would he?

But Noah veered backwards, lost his footing and crumpled down onto the pebbles, hitting his face against an iron girder.

Holly let out a cry.

Jay wiped his hand across his mouth.

Noah didn't move.

What now? thought Holly, close to tears.

Chapter 20
Deep Trouble

Jay shot Holly such an agonised look, it cut straight to her heart.

"So sorry babes," he said, his voice returning to that lovely husky tone. "I didn't mean to hurt your mate. Honest. I was dead scared when he came at me like that. He's OK, isn't he?"

Noah was sitting up now, his hand over his cheek and Holly could see he was very pale.

"He's only fourteen, like me," she said to Jay.

"Yeah, yeah, I know," muttered Jay. "Sorry mate. Lost my temper. Holly's my girl. She's like, so important to me."

He nodded down towards Noah, who gave a brief nod back.

Holly couldn't help feeling a thrill as Jay said 'my girl'.

But he did get nasty and throw that punch, she told herself. That's not right.

Jay pulled up his hood and muttered, "I'd better go."

Then he sprinted off up the beach to the road and was gone.

Holly stared after him, her heart sinking down through her body. Is it over, she thought? Will he go and find another girl? But why did he get so angry and throw that punch?

Her thoughts were a mass of confusion as she turned back to Noah.

She could see the grazed cheek now and pulling a tissue out of her pocket, she offered it, saying, "You OK?"

Noah didn't answer.

"What are you doing here?" she went on, feeling quite angry now. "You really upset Jay. That was our first date."

"He's too old – can't you see, Holly!" said Noah, dabbing his cheek.

Holly shook her head. "Don't be stupid," she said. "How did you know I'd be here, anyway?"

"You told Ellen and then she messaged me this morning. Becca messaged something about Jay."

"Becca Wilson? Are you mad?" Holly cried out. "She's jealous, she wants Jay for herself."

Noah frowned. There was a pause and then he went on in a more uncertain voice, "I didn't know that. But she says he's been messaging lots of girls and trying to get them to meet him."

Holly stared at him. Is that even true? she wondered. Becca's always stirring things at school. And look how Jay was prepared to fight Noah for me.

Or bully him? came a small voice in her head.

No, she told herself. That's not my Jay. He was just

spooked. He said so himself. Noah scared him, butting in like that when we were getting on so well.

Maybe it's Noah who's jealous. Jay thought so too, she told herself, telling Noah I'm his girl. She had to admit she liked that. Just not the part with the fists.

Can I forgive him? she thought.

Of course I can, she told herself. He was sticking up for his girl and things went a bit too far. He apologised to Noah very nicely.

"He's way too old for you, Holly," said Noah, breaking into her thoughts.

Holly looked over her shoulder for a moment at the sea. Then turning back, she smoothed down her jacket and ran her fingers through her hair.

"He's nineteen actually," she said.

"Exactly, five years older than you."

"I'm very mature for my age, Jay said so."

Noah shrugged.

"Look, Becca sent a Shoutout a while ago," Holly said. "She told us all to add Jay, said he was a nice guy. I know he messaged other girls but in the end it was me he wanted to be with."

"Why was Ellen worried then?"

"How should I know?" Holly stuck out her lower lip.

"And why did he try to punch me?"

"You scared him," said Holly. "He thought you were going to take me away from him."

"I think you should be careful about meeting him. It's lonely down here this time of the morning." Noah was brushing himself down as he spoke and then he let out a groan. "Oh God! Mum's going to kill me." He was fingering a large tear on the top pocket of his jacket.

Holly suddenly realised Noah was wearing a very smart suit and shot him a puzzled look.

"It's Ben's barmitzvah this morning," said Noah. "I should be at the synagogue. I'm going to be late and now I've torn my suit."

Holly couldn't help feeling sorry for him. He's had a shock too, she thought. My Jay's feeling just as bad. I'll go and find him but I'd better sort out Noah first of all.

"Come on," she said. "I'll get you there on time."

They trudged back up the steep pebbles to the road as a car screeched to a halt and Gideon and the twins threw themselves out onto the pavement.

"What are you doing here?" yelled Gideon. "Mum's going mad, what's happened to your face and look at your jacket." He gave Holly a brief nod.

Holly gazed round at the boys, waiting for Adam and Sam to say something mean as usual.

But to her surprise, Adam put his arm around Noah and said, "S'OK bruv. We're here now."

Adam seemed to know exactly what to do. "We'll switch jackets," he said. He and Sam helped to lever Noah out of the torn jacket and exchange it for Adam's.

"Won't you get into trouble?" asked Holly.

"Mum's used to me messing up," said Adam with a grin.

"Yeah," said Sam.

Gideon had found the first aid box in the car and put a plaster over Noah's grazed cheek.

Then Noah said, "I'm not going anywhere without Holly."

He gave her a meaningful stare and she frowned back. "I have to – um – get home," she said.

Noah shook his head. "Your mum and dad are out for the day, my mum told me and we saw some tattooed druggies wandering around the beach, right?"

He was staring hard at her and Holly knew if she didn't go along with him, he'd tell Gideon about Jay and the punch. Then maybe – she swallowed hard – Jay would get into trouble.

I need to speak to Jay on my own, she thought. Sort out why he got so angry. Once I get away from everyone, I'll message him to meet up at the café. It'll be fine, I know it will. He's my lovely Jay and we're supposed to be on a date today.

Gideon took charge. "We can't leave you here alone. Come with us, it'll be cool, OK?"

"Yeah, cool," said Sam and he gave her a kind smile. "Your mum would do the same for us..."

"...even if we're the Taurus Twins of Brighton..." put in Adam.

"I thought we were Leo, bruv," said Sam, with a puzzled frown.

"Don't sound as good."

Gideon grabbed Adam and Sam and pushing them into the car, snapped, "Shut up and let's get on with it."

He turned to Holly and in a kinder voice, said, "It sounds like you'd be safer with us."

Before Holly could protest, her mind in a whirl from all the events of the past half hour – it's only just gone ten, she thought, could so much have happened? – she was sitting in the front seat and Gideon was tearing off through town, coming to a halt ten minutes later and parking in a narrow side street.

"All out and move – come on, quick!" Gideon yelled

and they jumped out of the car, jogging behind Gideon to a large square building set back from the street.

"Our synagogue," Noah puffed to Holly.

Two men in fluorescent yellow jackets with walkie talkies nodded them through a high gate.

"Security," Adam muttered, catching Holly's eye as she raised her eyebrows.

"Keeping what secure?" she said.

"Us, you know, we're Jewish, lotta people got it in for us these days."

So why am I safer here? Holly wondered.

Her thoughts were cut off by a shrill voice – just like mum's, she couldn't help thinking – and a torrent of furious words pouring towards the twins and Noah. It was Linda Levy and her face was redder than Noah's ears when he was upset.

Gideon took Holly's elbow and steered her around his family and into a large hall which was almost full to bursting with people standing, sitting, calling to their friends, and pushing down the rows of seats to find places.

Noah caught up with them and said," Sit here, Holly. Look, there's Daniel."

Holly saw a tall man in his thirties, with fair hair, dark eyes and eyebrows, wearing a blue and white prayer shawl and a blue knitted skull cap.

So that's what a rabbi looks like, Holly thought.

They were sitting two rows from the front with Adam and Sam. Noah's parents and Gideon were further down the row.

Phone in hand, Holly just had time to think, Where's Jay? when Noah whispered, "Turn that off, OK?"

She pressed the off button and slipped the phone back in her pocket.

Suddenly the hall went quiet and everyone stood as the rabbi walked to the front and onto a low platform. He placed his hands on a wide reading desk and looked round at the congregation.

The service started and there was a lot of standing up and sitting down. Noah pointed to the right place in the book from time to time but Holly wasn't really concentrating.

Her mind kept drifting over the events of the morning. Where was Jay now? Maybe he'd messaged her. She'd have to find a quiet place soon and message back. Jay's last words rang through her mind. It wasn't all over, he still loved her. He was just spooked by Noah. He didn't mean to hurt anyone. The memory of their kiss on the beach came flooding back. He loves me, she told herself.

Noah gave her a nudge and she looked up. A boy, a bit taller than Noah, with wiry hair was standing next to the rabbi. Holly could see a white scroll laid open across the reading desk. The rabbi handed the boy a long silver pointer and the boy gave a nervous nod.

"Ben looks as scared as I felt last year," whispered Noah.

Holly gave a sympathetic grin. "I'd hate to stand up there with everyone watching."

"Yeah," said Noah. "And I had Adam and Sam sniggering in the front row. Mum and Dad didn't even notice." He gave a shake of his head.

"So is he reading all that stuff about not stealing, like you?" whispered Holly.

Noah shook his head. "It's a different portion. Ben's reading from Exodus 22. It's more about human rights, like how you shouldn't oppress refugees."

Holly nodded but then she slipped back into daydreaming about meeting Jay again. How long would he wait for her, even if he was in the café?

Jay will understand, she told herself. He knows me better than anyone. It'll all work out; just have to give the Levys the slip as soon as possible.

Noah nudged her and she saw that Ben had finished. Voices were calling out around the room and Noah said, "He did really well."

"Great. You must be – um - very proud."

Noah smiled and she knew she'd said the right thing. She leaned down the row and smiled at Linda Levy. But Linda frowned back.

Now what? wondered Holly, as she looked away.

Ben had re-joined his family and was kissing everyone in the front row.

If that was me, there'd hardly be anyone, would there? Just Mum and Dad and maybe Gran, if she felt well enough. She wasn't sure if the family would even come down from Aberdeen. They hardly ever met up. She felt a little pang of envy as she watched Ben move down the row.

When Ben finally sat down Adam and Noah thumped him so hard on the back his skull cap fell off and there was a fight to grab it and hand it back.

"Behave!" called out Linda down the row, a fierce look on her face and Noah's dad frowned.

"Idiots," said Noah, but he was grinning.

Having brothers doesn't always mean they're horrible

to you, Holly thought.

Noah had told her Adam was grounded for a week because of the ruined jacket. "It was big of him to take the blame, wasn't it?" he'd whispered to her in the service.

Who sticks up for me? she couldn't help thinking. Mum and Dad don't care anymore.

Jay would never let her down. Jay's always there for me.

His words on the beach came back to her. 'You're so gorgeous, babes. I'm so lucky.'

Finally the service was over and Holly walked out of the hall behind Noah looking around for the door to make a quick escape. But Noah steered her into another room.

Now what? she thought in despair. I really need to message Jay.

"Isn't it over yet?" she said in a low voice.

"Kiddish," muttered Noah and taking a small glass of what looked like apple juice from a tray, he handed it to Holly and said, "Don't drink it yet."

Holly shot him a puzzled glance and then the hall fell silent. The rabbi raised a silver cup and said a few words about how well Ben had done. Loud responses round the room and then everyone chanted what seemed to Holly another endless prayer.

She reached her hand into her pocket to reassure herself she could grab her phone the minute she was free. Jay will be really angry if I don't get in touch soon, she thought, shuffling her feet from side to side with impatience.

Finally, everyone drank from the little glasses and

then the rabbi handed a plaited loaf of bread to Ben.

"That's called challa," whispered Noah.

Holly let out a rather loud sigh and Noah frowned at her as Ben chanted a much shorter prayer.

As he finished, the room burst into loud chatter and everyone made for tables at the side, loaded with food.

Now's my chance, thought Holly. She swivelled her head round looking for the door, switching on her phone at the same time. But strangely there was no pinging of messages coming in.

Maybe the signal is bad in here, she told herself, as she walked away from the crowd and then Noah grabbed her arm.

"Mum and Dad want us." His ears had gone very red.

He pulled her into the corridor where his parents and Gideon were standing in a small tight group.

Holly had seen the twins make for the buffet but what did Noah's Mum and Dad want now? she wondered. It made her feel quite defiant. They're not my parents, she told herself.

"Well Holly," Linda started, folding her arms, "we were very concerned to hear you were on the beach this morning. Gideon says there were some bad people around. Your mum told me you would be at home all day studying."

Noah's dad nodded hard, his eyebrows raised,

Holly shrugged. "I felt like a walk." She put her head on one side and in a sulky voice, said, "All right if I go now?"

Linda's eyes narrowed but before she could speak, Noah said, "Holly was meeting a man."

Holly gasped. "Traitor," she hissed.

"I'm sorry, Holly, but I can't lie to Mum and Dad. Not after all that stuff with Rick." Noah ducked his head and then looking up he said, "Holly's been messaging a man called Jay and today she met him on the beach. He told her he was nineteen but I thought he looked much older. When I turned up he tried to punch me."

Linda's hand flew up to her mouth and Noah's dad took a step forward. "What man? Did he hurt your face? Where is he now? Tell me, son." His face was contorted with anger and worry.

Holly was horrified. "That's not true! My Jay would never hurt anyone and he's only nineteen."

"Then he's much too old for you, my girl. You're just a child," said Noah's dad.

"I'm nearly fifteen!"

"Speaking as a solicitor, Holly, I'm telling you that in the eyes of the law, you're still a child."

Holly gave a sulky snort. Who's he to call me a child? she thought.

"Your Mum and Dad will be absolutely horrified, Holly," said Linda in a worried voice.

No! thought Holly. They're not seriously going to tell Mum and Dad about Jay. All she wanted to do was run out of the synagogue but she was pinned up against a wall with Noah and his family standing in a semi-circle around her.

She glared round at the family, raging to herself. They're just like Mum and Dad. Never listen. Jay's the only person in the whole world who listens to anything I say. I can't believe that Noah betrayed me.

She was already working out the story she'd tell Mum and Dad when she got home; all about how nice

Jay is. She'd butter them up by saying he really wants to meet them. She still had a store of screen shots of some of their messages.

I can show them all the lovely things he's said to me, she thought. Noah's family haven't a clue and they've no right to judge me like this!

Noah's mum and dad were murmuring to each other and then to Gideon. Noah wouldn't meet her eye.

Then Linda said in a more motherly voice, "Holly, darling. We're very good friends with your parents, right?"

Holly gave a grudging nod.

"If anything happened to one of the boys, your mum and dad would want to keep them safe, wouldn't they?"

"S'pose," muttered Holly. "But I'm fine."

"Yes, we can see you are and Noah isn't hurt too much, thank goodness. But just like you helped Noah when Rick was bullying him…"

"…Yes!" cut in Noah's Dad, "That was fantastic, Holly. Really great."

Gideon muttered in agreement.

"So we have to make sure you're safe until your parents get home today," went on Linda. "We want you to stay with us and then Gideon will drive you home later. It's for the best darling. You'll have a nice time."

Linda and Noah's Dad fixed Holly with a hard stare and it was clear they expected an answer.

"Yes, fine," murmured Holly.

With satisfied nods, Noah's parents walked off and caught up with a group of adults. Noah slipped his hand on Holly's arm. "Still mates?" he said.

Holly shook his hand off and turned on him, "I can't

believe you did that! I should be the one to tell my parents about Jay, not your mum and dad. I didn't know your Dad's a solicitor, honestly Noah. It's so unfair!"

She flounced off down a corridor with no idea where she was going. Her insides were churning with anger and worry; about Mum and Dad but more than anything about Jay. She'd been checking and checking her phone and there were no messages. *We are private, don't tell anyone about us.* Jay's words rang in her ears. Will he ever trust me again?

Will Mum and Dad? came the echo back.

"Not that way." It was Noah and he ran round her to stand in her way, an anxious look on his face.

She stopped and tipping her head on one side, she stood there, arms folded, lips pursed.

"I'm sorry, Holly, but I couldn't..." Noah began, stuttering a bit. "I mean not after Ric..."

"...stuff Rick!" cut in Holly in her nastiest voice.

Noah's face fell and Holly was sure his eyes were welling up. He's just a school kid, she told herself with an inward sigh. Not a man, like my Jay.

There was nothing she could do for now while the Levys were in charge. She'd have to keep her head down and get away as soon as possible.

"All right, so what now," she said in a grudging voice.

Noah's face brightened a bit and he said, "Lunch and I have to do my speech. Adam said he's going to fart every time I stammer." He raised his eyebrows at her.

Holly couldn't help given a bit of a grin and they walked back down the corridor.

Noah showed her where she could hang her jacket and then they sat down at a large table with the twins and other kids from Ben's school. They had two courses and then it was time for the speeches.

Noah stood up, his ears flaming like traffic lights and managed to stammer only twice. Holly was terrified Adam would make a loud fart but fortunately he didn't seem to want any more trouble after the torn jacket.

Once Noah had finished and they were on the third course, Holly said, "Impressive."

"Just glad it's over," he muttered through a mouthful of chicken. "Never again! Anyway, that's the last barmitzvah in our family."

The afternoon passed quite quickly and then everyone was going home to get ready for the party in the evening.

Holly found a quiet corner, while Noah was talking to a friend and messaged Jay.

Holly: RUOK?? message me please jay
    : havent seen mum and dad yet
    : going to tell them all about you
    : I know they gonna luv you as much as me
    : you R such a nice boy jay
    : please please please message me
    : worried about U
But there was no answer.

His phone's out of juice, like last time, she kept telling herself as she swiped the screen, hoping for a message.

Gideon drove her home, Noah and the twins in the back again. Mum's car was already on the drive.

"Thanks for the lift," Holly said, as she stepped out.

Gideon drove off and Holly went to the door and let herself in.

Mum and Dad were standing in the hallway, frowns on their faces, arms folded.

Mum held out her hand. "Phone," was all she said.

Chapter 21
Grounded

"He's not a man; he's a teenager like me."

"Linda said Noah told her he's a man in his twenties," said Dad.

"Noah got it wrong. Jay's nineteen."

"You're not going out with someone aged nineteen!" shrieked Mum.

"Why not? I'm nearly fifteen!"

"Don't be ridiculous!" snapped Dad. "Your birthday was only last month."

It was past nine but it felt like midnight. Mum and Dad had been interrogating her for hours as if she was a criminal. How many more of these stupid questions?

They were all sitting at the kitchen table, Holly on one side; Mum and Dad opposite, so close together their shoulders were touching – like me and Jay on the beach, thought Holly.

They were taking it in turns to fire question after question. Holly just wanted to go to bed.

"How did you meet?"

"What do you know about him?"

"How do you know he didn't tell you a pack of lies?"

"Did he touch you on the beach?"

"Did he ask you to do anything you didn't want to do?"

Holly slumped back in her chair and rolled her eyes. How much longer do I have to sit here? she thought with an inward sigh.

"He's obviously a paedophile," snarled Dad. "Wait till I get my hands on him."

"He's not a paedophile!" Holly screamed.

"He sounds like one!" Mum screamed back.

"You're so STUPID!"

"Don't speak to me like that," said Mum, her eyes filling with tears.

Dad put his arm around her – really tightly, thought Holly.

Protectively.

Jay's the only person who wants to protect me.

But she couldn't help feeling sorry for Mum as she watched her wiping tears away with a finger. That made her look so –well – vulnerable.

There was a box of tissues on the counter and Holly reached behind her, grabbed the box and pushed it over.

Mum threw her a grateful glance.

Silence fell over the kitchen as if everyone had run out of breath. Dad pushed back his chair and went to put the kettle on. Mum reached out and patted Holly's arm.

But Holly flinched, jerking away.

They don't really care about me, she told herself, as she pushed her chair back and stood up to go.

They just care about what the neighbours say. Mum and Dad would rather listen to naggy Linda Levy than their own daughter and a hot rush of anger coursed through her.

"I'm going to my room," she said in a cold voice and put out her hand. "My phone, please."

Mum shook her head but it was Dad who answered. "We're keeping that."

He was staring at her with such a look of fear mixed with – well – deep disappointment on his face.

Holly stuck out her lower lip and without another word she went out of the kitchen and upstairs to her bedroom.

Pulling off her clothes, she put on her T and shorts and climbed under her duvet. Her head didn't have room for anything else today.

It'll be all right tomorrow, she told herself before she fell asleep.

Mum and Dad will calm down, I'll get my phone back. Then I can message Jay and we can meet up and sort all this out.

She woke up the next morning to raised voices in the bathroom. Mum sounded like she was talking through sobs and Dad's voice was edged with anger but Holly couldn't make out any words.

It was nearly nine. She'd slept for ages. What about Jay? she thought and reached out for her phone but then she remembered.

I'll get it back this morning, Holly told herself.

She rolled over to go back to sleep but there was a knock on the door and without waiting for her to call out, Dad came into the room.

"Time to get up, Holly. The police are coming at ten to see you," he said and disappeared before she could speak.

What!! Suddenly she was wide awake. Throwing herself out of bed, Holly ran downstairs and into the kitchen, saying in a strained voice, "Why are the police coming?"

Mum was standing at the sink, dabbing a tea cloth against her eyes.

"Don't upset your mother. She's had a terrible night," said Dad.

Holly hesitated and then she said, "Sor-*ree*... but I don't understand."

"We've called the police because you've been to meet a strange man on the beach," said Dad.

"You've been messaging him and we don't know who he is," said Mum.

For a moment Holly stared at them puzzled. What strange man?

Then she realised.

"You've got it all wrong. Jay's lovely and sweet and kind. Why do you want to get us into trouble with the police? Why?" Her voice was rising to a pitch.

What have they got against my Jay? They've never even met him.

"Enough of the backchat!" snapped Dad.

Holly stared at him in shock. He absolutely never spoke to her like that. Dad was always the one making a joke of everything. It was Mum who told her off.

But Dad was frowning at her now, standing close to Mum and suddenly Holly felt so utterly alone.

I need my Jay, she thought, tears welling in her eyes.

Without another word, she turned on her heel and went upstairs.

In her room she pulled on jeans and a long-sleeved T and sat down in front of the mirror. Her hair was a mess but she couldn't be bothered to straighten it. Mascara had smudged all around her eyes making her look like a panda. She'd been so tired last night she hadn't bothered to remove her make-up.

Running a finger over her lips she remembered how Jay had kissed her on the beach; the smell of his aftershave lingering in her nose.

If only I had my phone, she moaned to herself. Jay would listen to me. He always makes things right.

The doorbell rang. Men's voices sounded in the hallway – Dad's and another man and then a woman's voice, but not Mum's.

The police, she thought and a deep fear spread through her. She'd never so much as asked a policeman for the time. None of her family or anyone she knew had ever been in trouble with the police.

Noah had been shoplifting but the rabbi sorted it out. Noah's mum didn't report him to the police.

It's so unfair, she told herself.

Dad was calling to her to come down. It was too late to tidy up and anyway, her hands shook as she tried to brush her hair.

Will I be arrested because Jay's a few years older? she couldn't help thinking as she walked downstairs and into the front room.

A tall man in a suit, with grey hair – older than Dad, thought Holly – and a woman, with a slender figure, wearing a knee-length black skirt and jacket, were sitting side by side on the sofa.

Mum was sitting on one of the armchairs, looking as though she'd shrunk or something. Dad was standing next to her, hand on her shoulder. Mum had a tissue in her lap as she always seemed to these days.

"Hello Holly," said the woman. "I'm DC Katy Fielding and this is my colleague, DC Bob Jones. Why don't you sit down?"

Holly stood for a moment staring at them and then she dropped into the other armchair. Her chest felt even tighter than her throat. She looked over at Mum hoping for a smile but Mum wouldn't meet her eye.

The officers exchanged looks and the man took out a notebook and pen.

The woman held up a phone and said, "Is this yours, Holly?"

"Yes, I think so," said Holly.

It looks like mine, she thought. Why did Mum and Dad give it to the police?

"Can you tell me who's in this photo?" The woman showed Holly the screen.

Even across the room she could see it was the photo Jay had sent her.

"That's my boyfriend, Jay," she said.

Dad gave a loud snort.

"And is this who you met on the beach yesterday?" said the officer.

Should I tell them the photo is Jay's younger brother? Holly wondered but before she could decide, Dad was growling at her in a voice she'd never heard before.

"Come on, speak up. We haven't brought you up to

be rude to the police."

Holly stared at him in horror. Thanks a lot Dad! Now what will the officers think of me! she raged in her head. But she was too scared to snap back at him.

"Am I being arrested?" she said in a small voice.

The woman gave Holly the reassuring smile she'd so wanted from Mum and said, "Of course not, Holly. You haven't done anything wrong."

"This isn't your fault," the man joined in. He had a severe sort of face but his voice was just as kind as the woman's. "We're here to keep you safe. Your mum and dad contacted us because they're very worried about you, right?"

The man nodded towards Mum and Dad. Mum nodded back but Dad seemed to have frozen into a statue who just kept the same frowning look the whole time.

He hates me, thought Holly. At least I'm not going to be arrested.

She gave a shrug, puffed out her cheeks and said in a more casual voice, "That's a photo of my boyfriend. We've been messaging each other for ages and we decided to meet up on the beach yesterday."

Before the officer could say anything Mum cut in, her voice strained and shaky. "I don't know what's got into her. It's as though she's a completely different girl. She's so difficult these days, always flying off the handle whatever we say. We've never had any trouble from her before."

She paused and glanced up at Dad who shook his head and pursed his lips.

"She said she wanted to stay at home yesterday and

study for a test," Mum said, in a pleading sort of voice as if she wanted to make sure the police understood why she'd left Holly alone at home. "We've had to leave her for the past few weeks from time to time because her grandma hasn't been well. That's right, isn't it, Holly?"

Mum stared at Holly as if expecting her to agree but Holly looked away.

"You see," said Mum as if that proved everything she'd said was true. "You see how she behaves now. She never told us about a boyfriend. All these lies, we just don't understand it. Where's my lovely Holly gone?"

The woman nodded at Mum with a deeply sympathetic look on her face, as if she completely understood everything Mum was saying and believed every single word. The man was writing in his notebook.

I might as well not be here, Holly told herself. No-one's interested in me.

Then the woman said, "Do you understand why your parents are so worried, Holly?"

Holly didn't say anything but she could feel her face go red. Mum was being so embarrassing and no, the truth was, she didn't understand any of this. Why can't they give Jay a chance? she thought.

Mum opened her mouth but before she could launch into another rant, the woman said, "How old is the man you met on the beach?"

"Nineteen."

"Noah Levy, a boy in your school who also saw this man, claims he was much older."

"He was wrong," said Holly. "He made a mistake."

"Do you know Jay's last name or where he lives?"

"No."

"Aren't you curious?"

Holly gave an irritated sigh. "We only met for a short while before Noah came charging in. If I had my phone," she nodded at the phone in the woman's hand, "I could ask him, couldn't I?"

Dad gave an irritated tut but he didn't speak. The woman exchanged looks with the man again.

"Perhaps later," the woman said. "What sort of messages did Jay send you?"

"Read them yourself," muttered Holly.

Dad let out an angry snort and Mum shook her head with a sigh.

The woman nodded and said, "Well, they delete after a short while, don't they Holly? We just have a few screenshots, that's all. In fact we have been keeping an eye on the phone but Jay hasn't sent any messages in the past twenty-four hours. Doesn't that seem strange to you?"

"He had a problem with his phone a couple of days ago. He's probably fixing it."

She'd wondered herself of course why Jay hadn't messaged her back yesterday.

It doesn't mean anything, she'd told herself. He'll get back in touch when he can.

"Did he ever send you any photos or messages you didn't like?" the man suddenly asked.

Holly felt herself go bright red again and she stared down at her hands. This is so embarrassing, she thought. Why is he asking me that?

"Holly?" asked Dad.

"He didn't send anything…"

"Anything what?" asked the woman.

Oh God! thought Holly. What a nightmare.

"Anything rude!"

Even Dad's eyebrows shot up as she almost shouted out.

"He's not like that," Holly went on. "He'd never do anything like that."

The woman leaned over and murmured something to the man. Mum blew her nose and dabbed her eyes again.

Then the woman said, "We don't have any evidence that Holly has been the victim of anything inappropriate or against the law, at this stage. The messages have been deleted and the photo is clearly of a teenage boy about Holly's age."

Turning to Holly she fixed her with a hard stare. "Is there anything else you want to tell me?"

Holly shook her head.

"There are a lot of unpleasant men out there on the Internet," the woman went on. "You could put yourself at risk meeting someone you don't know; a stranger. For now we'll leave things with your parents. But if this man gets in touch again, Holly, let your parents know please, so that we can all help to keep you safe."

"OK," said Holly.

She felt weak with relief as they left. That was so humiliating, she told herself. Mum and Dad and the police assuming they know *everything* about me and Jay. As if I'd let myself be fooled by some paedo! Do they think I'm completely dumb?

Feeling more defiant now the police had gone, Holly strode into the kitchen. She couldn't remember the last time she'd eaten. Maybe she could wheedle Mum into making a big fry up.

She was rooting around in the fridge when her parents came in. As she turned they both leaned up against the counter. Dad had his arm around Mum and Mum was looking very pale, the shadows under her eyes even darker.

They seemed to be waiting for her to speak. She wasn't sure what to say so she said the one thing that had been on her mind all morning. "Can I have my phone back now?"

Mum shook her head as if in disbelief.

"No," said Dad.

"What! You can't take my phone!"

How would she contact Jay today? Arrange to meet up. Find out what he's thinking after yesterday on the beach.

"You don't seem to realise how serious this is, Holly," said Dad. "Those officers are from a special Child Protection Unit. They're quite sure that the man pretending to be this Jay is actually a paedophile…"

"…that's insane!" yelled Holly.

But Dad cut straight across her, "…and it's very clear he's managed to sweet talk you into believing you're in love with him. They advise us to keep your phone and your laptop…"

"…how am I going to do my homework?"

"And," went on Dad, still ignoring her, "You're grounded."

"Until when?"

"Until we know you can be trusted. You can do your homework on your mother's laptop in the kitchen, under our supervision."

"It's for your own good, darling," said Mum.

Holly stared at them in disbelief.

"That's so…" she was lost for words. "So… unfair! I hate you! You never listen, you're never here and you have no idea who I am or what matters to me!"

"You won't be left alone again, that's for sure," said Dad. "We want you straight home from school every day and either your mother or I will be here. We made a mistake trusting you alone in the house."

"We thought you understood about poor Gran, she's very disappointed in you," said Mum.

"What did you tell Gran for!"

"She's been worried about you ever since last Sunday when you went all rude and sulky," said Mum.

Holly shook her head, glaring at her parents. "I'm not your little girl anymore."

"That's very clear," said Dad in a cold voice.

Chapter 22
Our Secret

The rest of Sunday was miserable. Holly shut herself away in her room, lying on her bed, thinking of Jay. Dad came in and took away her laptop leaving a dusty empty space on her desk.

As she stared at the ceiling, she thought back to her fourteenth birthday, just a few weeks ago. The laptop had been her main present and she and Dad had set it up together.

As the screen lit up for the first time, Dad had said, "It's state of the art, Hol Pol. You could go to Mars with this piece of kit." He'd smiled at her in his warm, comfortable way.

"It's brilliant, thanks ever such a lot," she'd said and given him a big hug.

Now, lying on her bed with no way to contact Jay, she couldn't imagine ever hugging – or being hugged – by her parents again. They'd been so horrible to her in front of the police. It was almost as if they wanted to get her into trouble and why? What had she done wrong?

Fallen in love. That's all.

Jay's words were in her ears; *love you so much babes/ UR my girl/never gonna let anyone hurt U.*

She missed him so much she had an achy hollow feeling inside. She was sure he would be trying to message her today. How are we going to make up if I can't get in touch? she worried over and over to herself.

Dad called her down for lunch but she ignored him. She didn't want to sit and talk as though everything was normal.

I'll get a sandwich later, she told herself, even though her tummy was rumbling.

Half an hour later she heard Dad's heavy tread on the stairs and knocking on the door he came in and said, "Come down and do your homework, Holly. Mum's laptop's ready for you in the kitchen."

"Can't be bothered."

"Don't be silly. You don't want to get into trouble at school, do you?"

"*More* trouble, you mean," she bit back. "I'm already in trouble at home and with the police. Let's make it a triple whammy."

Dad shook his head as if he was tired of her but he didn't move, tapping a finger on the door handle as he stood there.

She gave an inward sigh. "OK, OK. I'll be down in a minute," she said, pulling herself up and pushing her tangled hair out of her eyes.

Dad left and Holly gathered up her books and went downstairs.

Mum was in the kitchen washing up. She gave Holly an encouraging smile. "I've put some lunch in the oven to keep warm, darling."

Holly ignored her.

Sitting at the kitchen table, laying out her books, Holly felt like she was in a prison cell with CCTV recording her every move. Mum's keyboard felt strange under her fingers and she had a headache – probably from starvation, she told herself. It was very difficult to concentrate.

If only Mum would go away.

But Mum spent most of the time leaning against the sink, a mug of coffee in her hand, staring at Holly.

Finally Holly couldn't stand it any longer. Pushing back her hair she stood up and said, "Finished," although she had hardly completed anything.

"That was quick," said Mum, her eyes narrowing with suspicion.

Holly shrugged and picking up her books, she went off up to her room. She stayed in her room for the rest of the day until bedtime. When she finally fell asleep, she had restless dreams of Jay, the police and her parents all meeting on the beach.

Monday morning Holly walked to school, her hands feeling empty without her phone. It was two days since she'd seen Jay or heard anything from him but it felt like months.

When she thought back to how excited and happy she'd been, looking forward to their first date, she could hardly believe how things had turned out. Her parents, the police, Noah's parents – everyone's against me, she told herself.

It was PE before lunch and the changing room

echoed with the shrieks and laughs of the other girls.

Holly slunk off into a corner to change. Ellen wasn't in her half of the year so she wouldn't be there. I bet Noah's told her and Tim all about Saturday, she thought, as she pulled on her shorts.

Madison's voice rose over the room. "You won't believe what Harry did on Saturday."

A clutch of girls huddled around. "Tell us," they pleaded.

Madison paused for effect.

Not another Harry story, Holly thought, with an inward groan. I can't stand it.

She looked around to escape but she'd have to push past the Bezzies and Aisha was bound to make some sort of remark. Leaning down, she laced up her trainers.

"So Harry likes rugby, as you know," Madison drawled.

Everyone hummed in agreement.

"So what he did – this is *so* funny." She let out a high-pitched laugh and Aisha giggled in her deeper voice.

Everyone laughed and exchanged looks.

Holly wanted to shriek, Who cares!

"He bought me – actually bought me – a rugby shirt. Can you believe it?"

"A girl's rugby shirt?" said someone in a puzzled voice.

Aisha and Madison rolled their eyes and the girl went bright red.

"No," said Madison, in an exaggerated tone. "It was a boy's shirt. Comes down to my knees. Harry said I looked sexy in it." She gazed through her long lashes around the room, expecting everyone to agree. There was a silence so she said quickly, "I was wearing leggings and a T of course."

"Course," said Aisha, glaring at everyone.

No one dared to speak.

Then Miss Holland came in and they all went into the gym for basketball.

Holly made sure she tripped up early and complained she'd hurt her ankle. Miss Holland told her to sit out.

Slumped on a bench, head down, staring at the floor, Holly wished she could disappear – from home, from school, even from Brighton. Amy had gone away. Maybe I should too, she thought.

"Penny for them?"

She looked up to see the teacher had sat down and was staring at her with a concerned look on her face.

"Nothing, Miss," said Holly.

Miss Holland nodded and then in a quiet, voice she said, "You know you can talk to me any time, Holly. My door's always open."

For a second Holly thought of blurting everything out as she stared back into the teacher's eyes, dark with concern.

Then an argument broke out on the court and Miss Holland threw herself to her feet and strode over, yelling at everyone.

After PE it was lunchtime but Holly couldn't face sitting with Noah, Ellen and Tim. They're bound to ask all sorts of questions, she told herself. Ellen will be mean and Noah and Tim will look embarrassed.

The corridor was very crowded as everyone pushed towards the dining room. Suddenly someone bumped into her from behind. Looking round, Holly saw Kelly E. She frowned and shrank back against the wall.

But the other girl leaned towards her and thrust a package into Holly's hands, saying in a low voice, "From Jay."

Their eyes locked for a second and Holly saw a flash of something again on Kelly's face – that strange, twisted look, like on the field with Becca. Then the other girl disappeared into the dining room.

Kelly E definitely knows my Jay, she thought. Why would he be interested in someone like that?

The girls' toilets were up ahead. She pushed open the door, went inside and into an empty cubicle. Locking the door, she turned the package over in her hand, a thrill going through her. Jay had found a way to reach her. But what had he sent?

Ripping off the paper she saw a phone nestling in bubble wrap. She stared at it, puzzled.

It's not my phone, was her first thought.

She took off the bubble wrap and switched it on. The screen came to life and messages streamed in.

It was Jay!

jay: RUOK??
　　: RU there??
　　: missing you so much babes
　　: wanna see you again very soon
　　: love you babes
　　: UR so sweet my beautiful holly

The messages went on and on and for the first time since they'd met on the beach on Saturday morning,

Holly felt wrapped in warmth. Jay was the only one in her world who really cared about her and he wasn't angry about Noah or anything. He was just missing her and worried about her.

holly: im here
: got the phone
: sorry about Saturday tried to message you

jay is typing...

jay: YAAAY!!
: cant tell you how much I missed you babes
: wanna see you so bad
: come to the beach after school
holly: cant im grounded
jay: bummer!! say you got a detention
holly: theyd ring the school and find out not true
jay: thats horrible
holly: they R!!!! so angry with them!!!
: they took my phone away
: sooo STUPID
: dont want me 2 have a boyfriend
jay: cos they R jealous
: too old for love
holly: yep
jay: hey i could come round tonite
: tell me where U live
: we could meet in the street late
: after they gone to bed
holly: dont think thats a good idea
jay: why not? dont U wanna meet

                : aint U missing me 2 babes??
holly: course I am but they would catch us
                : maybe tomorrow

A crowd of girls came in, laughing and calling out.
Holly unlocked the cubicle and went off down the
corridor. She found a side door, went outside and headed
for the field. It was a cold, drizzly day and no-one else was
about. As she walked her eyes were glued to the screen –
just like normal, she told herself with a happy sigh.

Jay said he was sorry he'd scared Noah and told her
how much he loved her – even more since they'd met.

jay: U can trust me holly
        : will never let U down
        : UR mine, all mine
        : UR my girl aint U??

It felt as though Jay's wide hazel eyes were staring at
her and his smiling mouth was warming her up as she
huddled in her jacket on the damp field. Her feet were
wet and her hands frozen but she'd never been so happy.

This is true love, she told herself. Me and Jay forever.

jay is typing...

jay   : did UR friend call police?
                : been worried about U
                : hope U didnt get into trouble babes
holly   : mum and dad did but its OK
jay: what did they ask U
holly: nothing much and anyway WHO CARES!!!!

jay: yep! we dont!!

holly: *smiley emoji*

jay: they dont know what we got U and me

   : its so special

holly: very special

jay: you gotta keep us private

   : thats why I got you a new phone

   : dont show UR mum and dad

   : they wanna split us up

holly: i know

    : wont let them

jay: love U so much babes

holly: love U2

jay: that's my girl!! U can trust me babes

   : never gonna hurt U

Holly grinned. She knew Jay would understand. So what if the police came round. That's the sort of thing parents do, she told herself. All those nights when I was home alone and so scared, no-one was worried about me then. But the minute I get a boyfriend, they want to control my whole life!

Jay understood and he's always there.

But there was still something puzzling her.

holly: kelly gave me this phone

jay: yep

holly: how do U know her

jay: she hangs with mikes sister

holly: oh

jay: what?

holly: kellys mean

: always in big trouble at school

jay: only way i could find U babes

: so desperate all weekend

: my head nearly exploded

:* sticker: boy frowning saying OUCH!!*

Holly laughed out loud and shook her head. Only Jay makes me laugh these days, she thought. If only Mum and Dad would give him a chance. He was so funny and lovely and sweet.

Jay was sending her more stickers when a voice called out, "Hey Holly."

It was Noah. Her heart sank but she couldn't avoid him. He was running over the wet field to catch her up.

"You OK?"

Holly nodded, her eyes glued to the screen.

"New phone?" asked Noah.

She looked over at him, his face creased in a puzzled frown.

"Um…yep. My phone broke so Dad lent me an old one of his."

Noah nodded. "So everything OK?"

"What do you mean?"

"At home, with your Mum and Dad? Everyone was worried about you on Saturday." Noah reached back and pulled his hood up.

"Even the twins?" she said in a mocking voice.

Noah grinned. "They're my brothers. They're allowed to tease me but they'd never let anyone bully me. We stick up for each other."

"OK," said Holly.

"Gideon kept saying, Should we call the police?"

"Oh God! No!" Noah's eyebrows shot up and Holly told herself to stay cool. Don't let him think anything is going on.

"Um – I mean, of course not. We don't need the police. It was all a mistake, that's all."

"Tim asked where you were at lunch."

"Mmm," said Holly not really listening.

"Sit with us tomorrow? Holly?"

Holly dragged her eyes away from the screen. "Yep."

They had walked back across the field and Noah was opening the outside door, waiting for her to go first.

Such a gentleman like my Jay, she couldn't help thinking.

"So is that Jay messaging you?" Noah asked.

Holly stopped for a second and looked around to see if anyone was listening. What if Mum and Dad found out about Jay's phone? They'd be bound to take it off her and now Noah was nosing around and asking so many awkward questions.

She shook her head. "He's gone away to stay with his gran in London. It's just Mum checking on me."

She rolled her eyes.

He fixed her with a stare for a second and then he said, "OK. You want to come over to mine for dinner tonight? Mum said you can come any night."

"Mum's expecting me home straight after school. Gran's Crisis is over," she said, forcing a smile.

"Cool," said Noah and he went off up a flight of stairs to class.

Holly switched off her phone and shoved it right to the bottom of her bag.

It's our secret, she told herself with an inward smile, as she went off to class.

Chapter 23
Like an Earthquake

"I don't need the laptop."

"How will you do your homework, darling?"

They were sitting in the kitchen having dinner. Mum and Dad had arrived home before Holly and she already felt suffocated. Funny how she'd never felt like that before. As Gran's Crisis got worse, she would have given anything for a normal family evening, eating dinner together and then watching TV before she started homework.

But that was before Jay, she thought.

"It's mostly reading. I can do it in my room – if that's OK." She glared at Mum.

"Of course it is, darling. You can always come down and use the laptop if you need it." Mum's voice was almost pleading her to say something nice back.

Holly gave a sigh. Why should I? she thought.

Dad put his knife down. "How was school today?" he asked, in a cool voice.

"Same old, same old."

"Did you see Noah?" asked Mum.

"Yep." At least she could answer that one honestly.

Dad sighed and said in a slightly warmer tone – not that much warmer, thought Holly, "You know we just want what's best for you. I can see you're still upset…"

"…what do you expect?" Holly cut in.

"We're your parents and it's up to us to decide what's best for you," said Dad.

Mum nodded, "Only what's best, darling," she said like a little echo.

Holly gave an audible sigh. I'm fed up with this, she thought.

She stood up and said, "I'm going to my room to study." She glared at Dad. "If that's OK with you."

Dad didn't say anything but he and Mum exchanged despairing looks.

Have they given up on me? she thought with a pang.

But as she walked upstairs all she could think was, now me and Jay can message all night.

holly: then dad said he decides like my whole life
jay: harsh
   : they dont know U
holly: yep
   : mum keeps nagging me about homework
   : SICK OF IT
jay: so sorry babes
   : wish I could see U
   : missing you so much
holly: me 2!!!
jay: hey!!! come over to mine
   : U can meet my friends
   : told everyone about U

: they R dying to meet U babes

Wow! thought Holly. He must really love me if he wants me to meet his friends. She imagined her and Jay cuddling up on the sofa in Jay's house, his arm around her shoulders, with all his friends sitting around.

Would we drink lager? she wondered. What would Mum and Dad say?

Who cares?

holly: would love 2 come
    : but still grounded
jay: we can work it out
    : trust me babes

The hours on her digital clock wound forward and Holly felt herself getting sleepy. She changed into her T and shorts and heard Mum and Dad coming up to bed. The house fell silent around her. She and Jay messaged until past two o'clock.

holly: getting sleepy
    : school in the morning
jay : OK babes

jay is typing...

Holly stared at the screen. Jay had sent over a photo of – well – his chest? The photo was from the neck down and he was lying on his bed with his top off, a line of hair down the bare skin. The button on his jeans was undone.

She felt quite shocked.

jay: cant stop thinking about how beautiful UR
   : how about a nice pic of U??
   : in UR bikini
holly: oh
    : dunno
jay: come on babes
   : only for me
   : U know how much I love U
holly: course I do

There was a long pause. Holly watched five minutes pass on the clock. Is he angry with me? She didn't know what to do and there wasn't anyone to ask.

What would Madison do? Harry had called her sexy in that rugby shirt. Does he ask her to send photos in her bikini? Holly wondered.

I could ask Madison quietly in school tomorrow, couldn't I? she told herself, feeling reassured. Madison would know what to do.

jay is typing...

jay: really want that pic babes
   : come on
   : U owe me dont U
   : UR mate came after me on the beach
   : UR parents called the police
   : its not fair
   : didnt do anything wrong, did i???
   : just one pic
   : come on babes
   : not much to ask is it???

He's right, she thought, feeling guilty.

It was all her fault Noah turned up. She shouldn't have told Ellen about meeting Jay and then Ellen couldn't have blabbed to Noah.

Jay said they were private and she shouldn't tell anyone. He was so right. And what if the police tracked Jay down and questioned him?

The thought made her feel even more guilty.

I couldn't bear to lose him now.

Life wouldn't be worth living without my Jay.

We love each other so much.

I want him to know I trust him completely.

She swiped through her photos until she found one Dad had taken when they went camping in the south of France last summer. Her bikini was OK – not that revealing, she told herself. Anyway, all those people on the beach saw me.

She clicked on the pic and sent it to Jay.

jay: awesome holly
   : UR so beautiful
   : UR a really good girl holly
   : such a good girl
   : my gorgeous girlfriend

Holly fell asleep with Jay's words ringing in her ears, such a good girl.

That's all she ever wanted to be, wasn't it?

The next morning she arrived at school to see Noah waiting for her by the gate.

"All right, Holly?" he called out.

Her eyes had been glued to the screen and now she stared at Noah, blinking.

"Yep."

"Your Mum texts you a lot," said Noah, as he fell into step beside her.

Holly looked up from the screen but she wasn't listening.

Jay had asked her all the way to school to come over to his place tonight. I can't keep refusing, she told herself. But how can I get away from the house?

"Holly?" said Noah in – well – a whiny sort of voice.

Why can't he leave her alone?

"Mum's worried about me now, she messages me all the time," Holly snapped at him.

Noah's dark eyes were staring at her and she could see he wasn't convinced.

"Have to go," she muttered.

She could feel Noah's eyes on her back as she walked away. He's so immature, she told herself.

Madison and the Bezzies were up ahead, swiping their phones and giggling.

She thought back to last night when she was so worried about sending Jay the pic in her bikini.

I can't believe I was actually going to ask Madison's advice, she told herself, suddenly feeling so much more grown up than anyone else.

My boyfriend's too old for school. He's a working man.

Switching off her phone, she put it in her bag and followed the others into class.

At lunchtime as she walked towards the outside door to

message Jay on the field, Noah appeared at her elbow.

"What now!" she growled, furious he wouldn't leave her alone.

"Just thought I'd walk around with you."

Holly pulled out her phone and switched it on. Jay's messages streamed down the screen.

"I don't want company," she said, shouldering the door open as a blast of freezing air hit her face.

She went out and walked as fast as she could towards the field, staring at the screen.

jay: what time U coming over babes??
holly: not sure i can get away
jay: sneak out
holly: mum and dad watch me all the time
jay: sneak out after they gone 2 bed
holly: maybe
jay: no
    : definitely

Holly paused, frowning at the screen. That's a bit much, she thought. What does he mean? Definitely. It's like – well – he's ordering me about or something.

She shook herself. Must be wrong, my Jay wouldn't speak to me like that.

jay: mean it holly
    : want you at my place tonight!

He sent the address. She could see it was a flat in a rundown part of town. Mum didn't like her to walk around alone in that area.

I thought Jay lived outside Brighton, she thought.

holly: not a safe area
    : cant come on my own
jay: get a taxi
   : want U 2 stay the night
holly: dont understand
jay: stay the night with me holly
   : U love me don't U??
holly: course
jay: what time U coming
holly: i dont think i can come tonight jay
      : im so sorry
jay: U will be
   : if U dont come

Holly stared at the screen. What's happening? Why is Jay being – well – horrible to me?

She re-read the message. Why does he want to make me sorry? For what? she wondered. Can't he understand Mum and Dad would never let me out after dark? I don't want to stay the night in his flat. Would his friends be there too?

Her mind whirled and whirled like a pin wheel but she couldn't make sense of anything.

jay is typing ...

jay: will tell UR parents the truth about us. They won't like what I have to say

What's he talking about?

She stopped walking and stared at the screen. Jay always said we were private. Is he saying he wants to meet them? Why is he talking to me like that?

It was as though Jay's voice – that lovely husky voice she heard on the beach – had completely changed. She could almost hear him snarling at her in the messages.

What have I done wrong?

If he tells Mum and Dad about us, it could ruin everything.

He must be muddled like me because of Noah turning up on the beach and Dad calling the police. Her fingers shaking, she typed back.

holly: what do you mean??
    : if you tell mum and dad now there will be so much trouble
    : dont understand
jay: I know where you live

What? thought Holly. I don't remember giving Jay my address. A chill was creeping through her and she glanced over her shoulder. It was almost like when she was home alone and every creak terrified her.

Why is Jay being like this?

holly: how do you know where I live?
jay: kelly knows
    : shes one of my girls
    : kelly does anything I tell her

What does that mean?

Kelly E is one of Jay's girls? Why would he want to

know such a horrible person? And what does it mean, one of *my* girls?

Does Jay have lots of girls and they do whatever he tells them? Or are they his sisters or cousins or something and he hadn't told her he had a big family?

Holly felt a stab of fear but she wasn't sure what she was afraid of.

Jay?

No, that's crazy, she told herself.

What's happened to my lovely Jay?

Nothing seemed to make sense anymore.

jay is typing...

jay : if U dont come over tonight

    : I will send kelly round to UR house

    : to tell UR parents about us

    : and that photo you sent me in UR bikini

    : I photoshopped it

    : you wont like it, trust me

    : i will post it on the Net

    : so everyone can see U

Holly froze in horror.

She couldn't believe what Jay was saying – no – threatening!

What's going on? What does he mean? Why is he doing this?

Her hands shook as she read and re-read the message, looking for some sort of explanation, something to show she was wrong.

He wants to post a photo of me all over the Net, she

thought, her mind grappling with the words.

What sort of photo?

And then with a sudden clarity she understood what Jay was really threatening.

Oh God! No!!!

Her body shuddered with panic as the image came into her mind.

Then everything spun out of focus as though an earthquake was shaking the ground beneath her feet. Staggering forward, her stomach heaved and she vomited over the field.

It can't be true! It CAN'T be! He can't mean it. Why would he do that to me?

Mum and Dad will see it all over the Net and they will NEVER understand. My life would be…

She wiped her hand across her mouth as her brain came to a complete halt for a few seconds.

Then it jerked back into action like an engine firing.

My life would be completely and utterly OVER!!

She retched again and again until there was nothing left to come up. Her stomach felt as if it was turning inside out.

Mum and Dad and Gran and EVERYONE will hate me for ever.

I might as well be DEAD!

As the horror of what was happening sank in, Holly felt her body go limp and fall forward… down, down, down, to a life she could not even begin to imagine.

Chapter 24
About Jay

Her knees crunched into a muddy puddle, small stones stabbing the skin and she cried out in pain. Then someone caught her arm before she fell forward onto her face. Hands grabbed under her shoulders but they couldn't heave her up.

If I stay down here in the mud, she thought, maybe I can just disappear, melt away like snow. No-one will ever know.

A frightened voice said, "Holly? What's happened?"

It was Noah. "Come on, get up. You're soaked and all covered with mud."

Noah's voice, panting with effort, pulled at her limp body. "Come on, help me Holly, that's it, push down with that foot."

Her head spinning, Holly slowly pushed herself upright.

She was soaked and covered in mud but what did it matter anymore? Nothing mattered. Her life was over. Jay – this man – had wrecked everything.

"Lean on me," Noah was saying and when she didn't

move, he lifted her arm and wrapped it over his thin shoulders. "What is it? You've gone all white." His voice was shaking.

Her phone was still in her hand and she stared at the screen.

"Is someone bullying you? Like me with Rick?" said Noah.

Holly couldn't speak, her throat frozen like her body. She read and re-read Jay's message.

It's all lies, she told herself.

Everything he's ever said to me was a lie.

Everything.

He's not who he said he was.

He's not my Jay.

He doesn't love me.

He's not my boyfriend.

I am so so… stupid.

jay is typing...

jay: come on holly answer me
   : cant wait forever
   : just wanna wakeup with U beside me
   : want my mates to meet U
   : U can trust me
   : i luv ya
   : gave U that perfume
   : expensive stuff
   : dont give it 2 all my girls
   : UR special

I don't know anything about him, she thought.

He's a liar and now I'm trapped!

I've been so stupid. Everyone was right – the police, Noah, Mum and Dad.

I've been trapped by a man on the Internet. Just like they warned us in school.

I thought they were so stupid and I was so clever.

She felt herself go weak again and leaned on Noah's shoulders. He staggered and took a step forward but managed to stay upright.

Thoughts rolled round and round in her mind.

Jay.

My Jay.

He's a... paedophile? Is he? Is that what he is?

And Kelly E, one of the worst people at school, is one of his girls.

Why is this happening to me?

Noah's voice was in her ear.

"Holly! What's going on? Tell me?" He sounded terrified.

Messages streamed down the screen getting more and more horrible until they were threatening things – well – she couldn't even imagine.

Then the photo she had been dreading appeared.

Noah was looking over her shoulder at the screen and he gasped. "God! Holly!"

She snatched the phone away and looked at him in horror. "That's not me, Noah! Please believe me. It's not me!"

Noah's ears had gone bright red and he could hardly meet her eyes. "I can't believe it... I... I..." His voice broke down in a kind of choking sound.

She shook her head hard, sick to the stomach again.

"It's not me, Noah. He Photoshopped my face onto… onto… Please believe me."

"Is that the man you met on the beach?"

She could hardly think straight let alone speak. How could he write those terrible words after all the lovely, kind, sweet things he'd said in hundreds and hundreds of messages?

Wake up, Holly! she felt like screaming to herself.

Only a liar and a paedophile would send such disgusting pictures and messages.

"Holly?" Noah said again in an insistent voice.

"Yes," she croaked. "That's the man you saw." She swallowed and licked the rain off her lips. Her mouth was dry and sour after vomiting. "He's not who I thought he was."

Saying it out loud to Noah felt so much worse.

"I've been so stupid. I can't believe it. He says I have to go to his place and stay the night."

"You can't do that!"

"He says if I don't he'll post that photo to the Net and everyone will see it. I couldn't bear it. Mum and Dad will throw me out. Gran might even die of a heart attack."

"That's blackmail."

"I know, he's trapped me." Tears poured down her face as she stood in the rain, the phone pressed against her jacket.

What can I do? I'm like a fly caught in a web and now Noah knows everything and he must absolutely HATE me. Nice, decent, honest Noah and his lovely family and his rabbi and all my family and everyone in the whole wide world will know how stupid I am.

I know NOTHING about… about Jay… the man… whoever he is.

"I'm the most stupid, thick, dumb person in the entire Universe!" she cried out.

Her ears were pounding and her eyes felt as though they could burst in her head.

"No, Holly. You're not," said Noah.

"Of course I am and I know you think so too. How could I believe he wanted to be my boyfriend? How could I be SO STUPID!!!"

"We have to tell somebody," said Noah in a hoarse voice.

"Are you mad? You mustn't say anything! Promise me!"

"I… I.. well…what are you going to do? You can't keep quiet about this. I'm going to the Head," said Noah. It was raining harder and his hair was plastered onto his head, water streaming down his face.

"No!!!!" she screamed out and she shoved Noah hard.

He swayed and nearly fell, but managed to stay on his feet. Stepping back a couple of paces he stood staring at her.

"Don't you get it, you idiot!" she screamed, as panic swept through her. "I have to go and meet Jay and do what he wants. I don't have a choice. If he posts that photo he'll ruin my life forever!"

But Noah still didn't move.

An almost white fury rose up through her. He's such a pathetic sort of boy! she raged inside herself as she stared at Noah standing there so bedraggled in the rain.

I need a rugby player like Madison's Harry to go over and punch Jay's lights out.

It was such a crazy thought she laughed out loud. I sound like a madwoman she thought in horror. Jay has driven me mad.

Then Noah shook his head hard and his hood, full of water, sprayed a cold shower over Holly's face.

For a moment she was blinded but as she blinked the water away, she saw Noah had moved closer. She stared at him, unable to move or speak for a moment.

Noah stared back, not blinking, as if willing her to… what?

Come down off the sea wall like when he went mad on the beach?

If I hadn't pulled him down, he could have been killed, she thought.

Is he trying to save me now?

As she stared into Noah's eyes, she suddenly had a deep longing for Amy. What would Amy say? One thing she knew for certain, Amy wouldn't abandon her now – just like Noah won't.

He's sticking by me like a loyal friend, she thought. That's what me and Amy would do for each other, isn't it?

"All right, Holly?" asked Noah, in his quiet voice.

She brushed her hand across her eyes and looked away down the field, her mind easing as her thoughts slowed down.

Why am I angry with Noah? This isn't his fault.

This is my fault. I made this mess.

I have to put it right.

That's what me and Amy would do for each other.

That's what I did for Noah when he was bullied.

I have to decide what to do and quickly.

Jay's dangerous. He really wants to hurt people – girls – like me.

He has to be stopped.

The bell for afternoon school sounded but neither of them moved. It was raining really hard now. Holly was shivering and soaking wet. All her limbs ached and she felt so weak. But she knew what she had to do.

"I'm not going to that man. I'm not going to see him," she said.

A look of relief crossed Noah's face. "Right. Let's go and tell a teacher."

For a minute Holly thought about Miss Holland. She'd guessed something was wrong.

No point, she told herself. There was only one place to go now.

"I'm going to the police."

"Yes! We'll go after school."

"No, Noah. You've been a brilliant friend..."

"...you did the same for me."

"Yes but this isn't like stealing a chocolate bar. I have to do this on my own and face up to it with Mum and Dad. Like you did all by yourself with your rabbi. That can't have been easy."

Noah ducked his head. "Worst thing I ever had to do," he muttered.

Holly nodded and set off across the field. Instead of walking into school, she went round to the gate which was automatically closing, ready to be locked for the afternoon.

Breaking into a run she managed to slip through in time.

Then she heard a voice behind her.

It was Noah and he was panting. He'd slipped through the gate too.

He put his hands up as she started to speak. "I'll just come to the door of the police station with you."

She hesitated and then nodded, relieved that she didn't have to go alone.

They caught a bus and sitting next to each other, Noah took her hand and held it until it was time to get off. It was so warm and comforting, she found it hard to let go once they were standing on the street.

"I'll come in with you," said Noah.

She took a long breath, trying to ease the panicky feeling inside. "No. Go home. I'll message you."

Noah hesitated and then he said, "Laters," – just like Tim, thought Holly – and it made them both smile.

He walked off as she crossed the street and up to the building, feeling more alone than ever in her entire life.

She pushed open a heavy glass door and saw a desk up ahead. A huge policeman was standing there, writing something on a piece of paper.

He looked up when she approached, looked back at the paper and said in a gruff voice, "Yes?"

Holly stood there, heart beating like a drum and then she said, "A man's doing something..." her voice cracked.

The policeman's looked up and fixed her with a serious look. "Yes, love? Someone after you?"

Holly nodded and she felt tears start again in her eyes.

She shook them away. No, she thought. I'm not going to do it like that and sticking out her lower lip, she said,

"A man's been threatening me."

Then she pulled out her phone, found the photos and showed them to the policeman, swiping through as her hands shook and shook.

The policeman stared at the phone, his expression unchanging – does he believe me? thought Holly – and then he said, "I'm going to call someone, love. You wait right here. Don't move. OK?"

She could have hugged him with relief.

After a few moments a door at the end of the reception area opened and Holly saw the woman police officer who had come to their house. She had a concerned look on her face and in a soft voice, she said, "Can I help you Holly?"

Holly nodded and said, "I've come to tell you about Jay."

Chapter 25
Holly's Diary: Extracts

Feb 26th

Jay was arrested this evening!! They grabbed his computer and phone as well. He never had a chance to post that horrible photo. He's in prison and I'm safe.

Feb 27th

How could I be so wrong??!!?? DC Katy Fielding came round this morning. Jay's been released on bail. UNBELIEVABLE!! I just don't get it.

My stomach heaved and I was sick in the toilet. Mum's in bits. She can't stop crying. Dad storms round the house looking mad and clenching his fists.

DC Katy said there won't be a trial for months. If it even gets to trial. Dad shouted and Mum put her hands over her ears.

I hate it, all the trouble I've made. Poor Mum and Dad. It's so unfair.

I thought nothing could get worse but it just did.

2:30am

It's the middle of the night. I can't sleep. Me and Jay used to message all night and I know it's mad but I can't stop thinking about him. I mean what if he came round and said he was sorry and it was all a big mistake and he didn't mean anything bad and he really DOES love me. What would Mum and Dad say? Or DC Katy?

March 1st

Read through my diary. Am I totally stupid? Jay never loved me. He wanted to hurt me. Dad keeps saying it over and over again as if he can read my mind. Truth is, Jay is free to walk around Brighton and I'm too scared to get out of bed.

I'm the one who's ended up in prison.

But if only I could speak to him. Just once. Tell him how bad everything is. Just once.

March 2nd

In bed all day.

March 3rd

Mum came up. She said Ellen, Tim and Noah are downstairs. I told her to tell them to go away. I feel such a mess. What would Sandi say? I can't go on YouTube anymore. I don't have a phone or a laptop. I'll NEVER go on the Net again.

March 4th

Everyone knows. I'm sure they do. It's gone round the whole school. I'm positive. They're all laughing at me. I can almost hear them.

March 6th

Haven't left my room. Mum and Dad keep coming up and bringing me treats and trying to talk to me but I can't tell them how I really feel. Like I'm going mad. It would make them even more sad if that's possible.

Today they said we're all going to Gran's for lunch. I was so terrified at the thought of leaving the house with Jay out there prowling around, I couldn't even speak. I just screamed at them!!! Opened my mouth and screamed. Mum went out sobbing. I'm making things worse. I'm so USELESS.

I'm really scared I'm going out of my mind. I don't know what to do and I can't tell Mum and Dad. They've been so AWESOME. I don't deserve it. They should be shouting at me.

Nothing feels the same anymore.

March 9th

I'm so ashamed of myself and everything I've done and I feel so totally guilty. Everyone thinks I'm so stupid, I know they do - Mum and Dad, DC Katy, all my friends – my former friends – no-one wants to be my friend anymore, I'm absolutely certain.

It feels like the whole world is laughing at me. Mum cries almost all the time. Dad keeps telling me it wasn't my fault. Jay's the one to blame.

It doesn't help.

Nothing helps.

March 10th

Miss Holland came round. I was downstairs getting a drink of water and Mum brought her in the kitchen so I couldn't escape upstairs. Miss Holland went on and on about how she felt guilty she hadn't made me come and talk to her. She knew something was wrong.

She gave Mum a leaflet, for children like me who have been abused, she said. I wasn't listening after that because all I could think was, 'Did my Jay abuse me?'

But Mum looked sort of brighter after Miss Holland left and she rang the number and I couldn't say I don't want her to because I feel so bad. I'm desperate for Mum and Dad to feel better.

Someone's coming round tomorrow. A counsellor. Her name's Karen.

June 12th

Four months since Jay first messaged me. I've been seeing Karen every week. We talked about my diary today so I came home and found it at the back of the drawer. It made me feel sad reading back through it but now I've started writing again on a clean page – with a purple pen, I like purple – I think I'll go on.

Karen knows how to listen without telling me off or being stupidly pitying and never ever cries whatever I say. She thinks writing in my diary will be helpful. I can sort my thoughts out and read them back.

I go to her office every Wednesday. The room smells of new carpet and she has these lamps which give everything a soft glow.

Karen's about Mum's age I think and she wears a wedding ring so she must be married. But she never tells me anything about herself.

This space is for you, Holly, she says.

I like that.

Jay said we were completely private and I could trust him and not anyone else. Not Mum or Dad or my friends at school. He tried to get me away from anyone who loved me or cared about me.

They call it grooming when a man sucks you in like that and then threatens you until you do what he says. Dad said he sweet talked me. Dad was so right and I didn't listen. I only listened to Jay.

But the truth is I've been groomed by a paedophile on the Internet. It makes me feel so empty inside. I'm not too-young Holly anymore. I feel older than all the girls in school.

Karen says everything I say in her room is confidential and she won't tell anyone.

I can tell people if I want to. It's my choice.

Karen doesn't keep telling me I can trust her.

I just know I can.

I've written a whole page!

June 13th

I've read through yesterday and it feels good having all this on paper. I know now that everything Jay said was a lie. Every single word!!

But it was like he was tattooed on my brain. I couldn't stop loving him even after I found out the real truth about him. I couldn't understand it.

Karen says it's not unusual to go on having feelings for the groomer even when he's found out. That explains why I missed being able to message Jay and tell him everything and why I was still in love with him for ages after.

Karen asked me weeks ago if Mum and Dad still hug me. I went all cold inside. She said people who are groomed are often people who aren't touched very much. I told Mum and she cried so much I wished I hadn't said anything. But ever since she and Dad hug me all the time.

Which is really nice.

Dad keeps saying how he was busy with work and they were worried about Gran and they took their eye off the ball and so I got hurt.

It's true they were too busy for me.

But I should have told them how scared I was home alone.

And I was an utter idiot to let myself be groomed by a paedophile on the Net.

But Mum and Dad are much better since I've been seeing Karen. They didn't know what to say to me but Karen does because she's a trained counsellor.

Karen says, 'You can't change the past. But you can change your relationship with it'. She says I can learn to forgive myself and not see myself as so stupid.

I hope so.

June 18th.

I still feel stupid.

But it does help to write it down. Sort of makes things more real.

So here is the horrible truth in black and white – well, purple. Still using my favourite purple pen.

Jay is really called Frank Taylor and he's 26 years old.

How could I have been so stupid to believe he was only nineteen???!!

DC Katy Fielding said he looked young for his age but Noah could see straight away. I was blinded by love and all the lies Jay told me.

He manipulated me to make me fall in love with him. Then he set the trap and blackmailed me.

Frank Taylor used the photo of his fourteen-year-old brother to lure me into his trap. How sick is that!

We exchanged over 2000 messages in ten days. That's why I felt I'd known him for months. He never let me go, messaging all day and all night.

DC Katy said some girls meet their groomer the day after the first message. I wouldn't have done that. But I still got taken in.

Looking back all the warning signs were there.

He never told me anything about himself.

But every time I told him something – like my favourite colour or hating animals – he said he was exactly the same. It was all about creating the trap. Making me believe we were in love and we had so much in common.

If Noah hadn't found me on the field that day, would I have gone to Jay?

Yes, I think I would.

I was so terrified.

My breathing's gone a bit funny. Can't write anymore.

June 21st

Haven't written for a week. Mum just brought

up my fave chocolate bar and I've finished my homework. So here goes.

Mum and Dad have been AWESOME. UTTERLY AWESOME.

They never go on about how horrible I was to them and even to poor Gran. They told me they could see I was changing but they couldn't understand why. They must have been so scared and I didn't think about them once.

The worst thing now is the waiting. Waiting for a trial date. Waiting even to see if there will be a trial date. I'm so scared of going outside on my own in case Jay/Frank is there. What if he grabs me in the street or tries to make me go with him?

Dad says, try not to think about it and Mum says, we won't let him near you ever again.

But when I'm alone in my bed at night I imagine all the things that could have happened.

I didn't go to school for three whole weeks after Jay was arrested and then let out on bail. I know he has all sorts of injunctions to stop him going near me but can that really stop him? I kept imagining what I would do if I bumped into him in the street or the Mall.

In the end I decided I want to get my exams like everyone else. But the minute I walked into school it was obvious straight away that everyone knew what I did. I think Becca spread it around. I had sneers and stupid jokes and even poisonous messages stuffed in my locker.

It was terrible but I didn't have to face it alone.

I'm very lucky to have good friends. I don't deserve them.

Mum or Dad take me to school every single day. Tim and Ellen and Noah make sure I'm never alone and I go home every day with Noah so I'm not on my own in the streets. My friends have been AMAZING!! They never make me feel like an idiot. We're a proper crowd now like I wanted for ages. We sit together at lunch and walk out of school together. When people make stupid comments Ellen gives them her mean stare and they soon back off.

Kelly ended up in foster care far away from Brighton. The police found out Jay was making her do horrible things. She doesn't have awesome parents like me. I sort of feel sorry for her but I'm glad she's gone. She's way more nasty than Becca.

Madison and Aisha have been great too. They keep coming over and linking arms and telling me I'm a nice girl and they still like me.

I need it so much.

I need to hear it all the time, every day.

Because deep down I don't really believe it.

Nice girls – like Ellen and Madison and Aisha and Amy – they don't let themselves be taken in by paedophiles, do they?...

December 19th

We are in the airport waiting for our plane to CANADA!!!!!!!

We're going to spend Christmas with Amy and her family. I can't wait to see all that snow. Amy's promised to teach me to snowboard.

Amy and me are best friends again. She was utterly brilliant after Jay. I didn't have a phone. Mum and Dad and DC Katy thought it was better if I wasn't on the Net for a while. I talked about it with Karen and I realised I didn't care. I was actually scared of the Internet after Jay.

So Amy rang me all the time on the landline. She was so sorry about sending me pics of sleepovers and Gabe. She didn't want me to know how hard it was for her to move to a new country so she pretended she was having a good time. She never thought it would upset me.

Amy says Jay would never have stood a chance if she'd been there. Well of course if she hadn't gone away, I wouldn't have been so lonely and Jay would never have got hold of me. But it's not Amy's fault. It's mine.

When she wasn't phoning me Amy sent me funny postcards and it was great to keep getting mail. Sometimes she sent me little presents like Peanut Butter chocolate bars which are weird. Can't wait to see her.

But mostly I can't wait to get away from Brighton and Jay/Frank. I keep imagining he's standing under the tree outside our house, staring up at my window. Or he's sitting upstairs on the bus when Noah and me go home from school. He could be lurking round every corner.

I hope I can forget all about Jay/Frank for the whole time.

We're staying until the New Year and then Amy is coming to us in the Easter holidays. We'll always be best friends, Amy said.

I asked her if she still watched Sandi's YouTube channel.

'Course I do!!' she said.

April 3rd

It's fourteen months since Jay first messaged me. The nightmare is finally over. We had the trial and it was as horrible as I thought it would be. I had to give evidence by video link. The defence cross-examined me and they tried to make out it was all my fault for chasing after Jay/Frank.

As if!!

It lasted for three days and I couldn't eat the whole time. It was like there was a huge lump in my throat. Mum made me drink full-sugar cola to keep my strength up. It's disgusting. I only ever drink diet sodas.

In the end it didn't matter what the defence lawyer said. The jury took 45 minutes to come to a decision.

Guilty!!

It's really and truly over. Frank Taylor has gone to prison. I wasn't his only victim and I don't want to write down here all the things they found out he'd done to loads of other girls. But the judge gave him eight years and my lawyer was very pleased.

I still feel strange walking around Brighton without Noah or Mum or someone with me. I'm not used to not feeling scared all the time. But I missed the freedom so much. The weather's warmer and last Saturday I went down to the beach for a few minutes by myself. Then I went to meet Ellen in the Mall to go shopping. It felt so good to be out on my own at last.

I'll be a grown up in my twenties when Frank Taylor comes out of prison and he won't be able to touch me, as Ellen says with her meanest glare. It makes me laugh.

I was fourteen when Frank Taylor found me on my phone. I'm fifteen now. Everyone is talking about college and courses and what they want to do. Ellen still wants to be a veterinary nurse and I'd like to be a teacher. Mum says she's pleased I'm looking forward.

I couldn't bear to do that the whole time Frank Taylor was out on bail, or when the trial was going on, or waiting for the sentence.

But there is really nothing to be scared about now.

So long as I'm sensible.

I still see Karen and sometimes I still tell her how stupid I was. But not quite so much these days. Since Frank Taylor went to prison I feel different. I can feel things begin to shift inside me like Karen said they would. I am beginning to move on and to forgive myself.

Noah and me have become good friends. He still holds my hand sometimes. We go up to Tim's place – he and Ellen are proper in love – and I'm still not keen on animals but I quite like collecting eggs from the chicken coops.

Noah and me never talk about that day on the field. We just know. But sometimes I catch him looking at me and I think, I'm really glad he was there that day.

Noah says a true friend sticks by you in the bad times; not just the good times. Like I did on the pier for him when he was in such a terrible state. He says he was lucky to have a good friend like me that day. That feels nice.

Amy says the Internet is a good place and a bad place and she says my experience has made her much more wary. She's right. The Internet can be fun. I have a phone and a laptop again and I go on social media like everyone else.

But you have to be careful. Lots of kids – like me – would never speak to a stranger in the street. But they don't think twice – like me – about telling a stranger everything about themselves on social media.

Karen says, It will get better.

Miss Holland says, Come and talk to me if you're worried about anything.

Madison says, Harry's gorgeous and we all sigh.

I have my friends and family to keep me safe.

I will never make the same mistake again.

Author's Note

The Internet is a fun place and like many people, I enjoy using social media. But it is important to be aware of the dangers and to keep yourself safe. I was compelled to write this book because of two heart-breaking cases I read in the newspapers; two teens who were both groomed by men on the Internet and sadly lost their lives. The girl was fifteen and met her groomer on Facebook. The boy was approached by his groomer when playing online computer games. Both boys and girls can be vulnerable to being groomed. This story shows how this might happen to readers or to someone they know.

If you are worried either for yourself or for someone else, then this is what you can do:-

1. Tell a teacher
2. Tell a parent/carer/ older brother or sister
3. Tell the police
4. Contact ChildLine: https://www.childline.org.uk/ Tel: 0800 1111 (calls are free)

5. Contact ThinkUKnow: https://www.ceop.police.uk/ceop-reporting

6. Contact ChildNet: http://www.childnet.com

For this book I consulted professionals in both the public and voluntary sectors for background information, as well as reading case studies and stories online and in the press. I would like to especially thank Steve Harris, Child Protection Officer, for his invaluable input about child online grooming.

Lynda Hamitouche, Jessica Clarke, Chloe Marlow and Kelly Marlow, students at Friern Barnet Secondary School, kindly formed the core of a focus group. We met for several sessions over a year and the group helped me to understand how they use social media and how Holly might meet Jay. My thanks to all the girls for their advice and support. I was particularly impressed by their understanding of the possible dangers on the Internet and their cautious and sensible approach to social media.

My heartfelt thanks to my agent, Anne Clark, who supported this book from the first outline and to Elaine Bousfield at Zuntold, who felt that this was an important story to publish.

Miriam Halahmy
www.miriamhalahmy.com

For other insightful books,

head to

Zuntold.com